Night Walk

and Other Dark Paths

Aeryn Rudel

The Molotov Cocktail

Portland, Oregon

Contents

Dusk

Midnight

Dawn

Foreword

Horror renders the familiar as uncanny. It imbues everyday occurrences with unrelenting dread. In the right hands, it's a genre that reveals our basest impulses by evoking the most elemental of responses: fear.

Aeryn Rudel's horror doesn't shy away from the familiar; these pages abound with classic ghouls. *Night Walk* ripples with the ghastly handiwork of bloodsuckers and wolfmen, demons and serial killers, beasts that skulk through the dark and even simply the darkness itself. But while you may recognize their trappings, these monsters slink down unpredictable paths in a flash fiction collection where nothing is at it seems.

Throughout *Night Walk*, Rudel places desperate characters in utterly bleak situations, and the twisted joy of poring over these pages can be found in discovering which characters give in to the inevitable and which are more prone to gnaw off a leg to wrench themselves free. Whether by leading a lamb to slaughter in "The Ruins by the Woods" or dispatching droves of man's best friend in "The Father of Terror," characters are often compelled into the grisly business of shedding innocent blood to keep more powerful forces at bay. Elsewhere, such as in the frigid wasteland of "Simulacra" or the sun-scorched cross-continent trek in "Toward the Sun," haggard survivors face their impending ends with eyes wide open.

For every story where barely contained sinister forces lurk just along the periphery, as in the title piece, there is one in which unfettered malevolence pours from within, as with the macabre artist found in "The Sitting Room." And in stories like "Stall Number Two" or "The Rarest Cut," it's an unsavory compulsion that leads characters to whittle away at their own bodies and souls.

Throughout these disparate stories, Rudel weaves a common thread of human connection—and the consequences that spring forth from a lack thereof. That's done quite literally in the entangled body horror of "What Binds Us" or the mind-meld between a little girl and a hungry lump of animate flesh in "Little Sister." Human connection is rendered more subtly and poignantly through the eyes of a lupine predator in "Two Legs," while neither land nor sea can keep a family apart in "Reunion." Meanwhile, it's the connective tissue of memory for what his family once was that fuels a young boy to bravely confront what they've become in the devastating "Where They Belong." You'll also find humans bound to the unnatural, such as the abominable crop poking up through the soil in "Things That Grow" or the carnivorous trees of "The Grove."

Rudel's dark and offbeat fiction first caught our eye at *The Molotov Cocktail* many years ago with a little piece about a futile attempt to hold oneself together in "At the Seams," first published in 2014. Since that time, we've been privileged to publish over a dozen of his stories, and he's the only writer to be featured in all five of our anthologies. With *Night Walk*, we're thrilled to present 40 of his very best pieces of flash fiction. Dive in and don't look back.

Josh Goller
The Molotov Cocktail
April 2021

Part I
Dusk

Things That Grow

I remember the old men and women who gathered at Hodge's Feed talking about Mr. Wilmot. They'd go from near shouting about the weather or the Atlanta Braves to whispers and furtive glances when his name came up. It was always the same: he never married, his farm had been in the family for generations, and his fields were ripe even in the winter. They never said he had a green thumb or even that his crops were bountiful or lucrative. Instead, one of the old-timers would take a pull of the hooch Mr. Hodges brewed in his cellar and say something like, "It ain't natural, but that man has a way with things that grow."

When I was nine, I asked Dad what they meant.

"Hush now, Matthew," he'd said. "That's grown-up talk." I recall he whispered, like they did, and was careful not to say the man's name.

The feed store wasn't the only place people talked about Mr. Wilmot and his big farm in the middle of nowhere. When I was a freshman, some of the older kids would say things. A conversation between two of the popular boys, Danny Boyd and Justin Goddard, stands out.

"He ain't never had no kids," Danny said, his freckled face serious and knowing, like the old folks at the feed store. "None that lived."

"My daddy said he steals babies and gives them to the devil," Justin replied, his eyes twinkling with ugly mirth.

He was an oily, short-tempered kid, mean and brutish. Danny wrinkled his nose, like Justin's words smelled as bad as they sounded. "Your daddy's a drunk, and I don't know nothin' about what he said, but I know Mr. Wilmot's fields make noise."

"What do you mean?" I asked, that tempting bit of information giving me the courage to do more than listen.

Danny regarded me the way you might a broke-leg dog. "One time we drove out there. Me and Justin. We heard it."

The nastiness on Justin's face faded, and something more fearful took root. "Yeah, like babies crying."

A few years later, when I had a car of my own and more bravery than sense, I drove out to Mr. Wilmot's farm. The dirt road to his property split off Route 57, and trees—great big things that swayed in the dark—crowded on all sides. I stopped the car about a mile from his place.

I got out, stood in the dark, and listened. I smoked one cigarette and then another to calm my nerves. The wind whispered in the trees, the frogs and crickets made their soft ruckus, and then, at the edge of what I could rightly hear, an unmistakable sound. There's something different about how a newborn baby cries, a halting, hitching thing, plaintive and a little frightening. I heard that beneath the wind, up the road.

I should have turned back, but I wanted to know why the old folks talked about Mr. Wilmot in hushed tones, and why the mention of his fields could unsettle a mean-spirited asshole like Justin Goddard.

I walked down the road until Mr. Wilmot's barn, black beneath the staring eye of the moon, loomed ahead. Tall rows of corn stalks thrust up near the structure, but next to the road, something else. Plump, bulbous things sprouted from the earth beneath twisting vines.

Those hitching cries came from the ground, and my blood froze, but I had to see.

I hopped a rickety wooden fence and my feet sunk into the soft earth on the other side, moist as a newly irrigated field. My shoes squished in the muck as I approached the swollen shapes on the ground.

I thought they were pumpkins or gourds, and they might have been at one time. It was so dark, I couldn't make out much, but that pitiful newborn squalling rose up around me, louder, more insistent. I pulled out my lighter, thumbed it to life, and bent close to the ground.

My head spun from all the noise, the awful cries of Mr. Wilmot's field, but I held the lighter up to one of the gourds. Its color was wrong, more pink than yellow or orange. The surface was smooth, unblemished, and I could hear it wailing, slightly muffled. I reached out and touched the thing. Its warmth made me cringe, but I rolled it over.

There, scrunched up on that fat gourd was the face of a newborn baby with an open mouth and black eyes. Freed from the dirt, it loosed a terrible, howling shriek. I fell backward on my ass and dropped the lighter. The cries around me grew louder, desperate, a chorus of monsters screaming for their father.

A light came on in the barn, and I hightailed it to my car and raced back to town. I never spoke of it to anyone, not my father, not even the old folks at the feed store.

That was five years ago, and only now have I worked up the courage to return. They don't talk about Mr. Wilmot's strange agricultural skill any longer at Hodge's Feed. They talk about people and animals disappearing near his farm, of darting shadows in the moonlight, and a new crop, more terrible than any before.

I'm standing on that dark road of Route 57, two cans of kerosene at my feet, my pockets stuffed with road flares. I don't hear the wails of newborns. I hear the squeals of children, their voices high and piercing. There are no words, but I know they talk to each other and to their father in the black barn under the moon.

He has a way with things that grow, they said. I will burn it all before more of Mr. Wilmot's children slip their vines and the rotten earth that made them.

Shadow Can

When I was little, my shadow scared me something fierce. Mama said I was right to be afraid. She told me your shadow is a dark reflection, an almost-invisible demon bound to your fleshy self. She said it was a collection of all the ugly things about you, all the bad thoughts you don't act on but still think about. I grew up, and I stopped being afraid. I thought Mama was just spinning some of that Louisiana hoodoo she grew up with to scare us. I should have believed her.

It started one long July afternoon. I lay on my bed, sweating like a bastard in the sticky Louisiana summer while wearing nothing but undershorts and my sweat-slicked skin. My shadow flickered and moved across the ceiling as the sun streamed into my tiny bedroom.

Maybe it was some kind of heat daze, or maybe it was the pot I'd smoked the night before with Tommy Nelson across the hall, but a strange thought popped into my head—I should tell my shadow to do something, to get me something I wanted. I pointed at the ceiling where my shadow hung like a cool spot of shade just out of reach. "Shadow, get me a Coke."

My shadow didn't do shit, and I laughed at the silliness of the thing, turned over, and fell asleep despite the murderous heat. When I woke up a few hours later, a bottle of Coke sat on my rickety old nightstand. It was the most beautiful and terrifying thing I'd ever seen.

The room had grown darker in the late afternoon, and

the shadows had thickened. I saw *my* shadow against the far wall, opposite where it should be from how the light came in through the window. It waited, unmoving, a blot of eager darkness on the white plaster. Its head—my head, I guess—moved a bit, a nod maybe. That's all it took.

Over the next couple of weeks, I learned what my shadow could do. It could bring me things, and not just sodas from the liquor store. It could bring me the cash out of the liquor store's register. It could bring me that new pistol I wanted at the pawn shop. I just had to make sure there was enough light, and when my shadow appeared on the wall, I just told it what to do. "Shadow, bring me this. Shadow, get me that."

I think acknowledging it like I did made it free, admitting it had a mind of its own gave it power. The Wilsons' cat, Ralph, died first. He sometimes came into my room in the morning and slept on my bed. I liked that little furball. My shadow knew that—it knows everything about me. I found Ralph on the foot of my bed a week ago, still and ice cold. His eyes were black, like the life had been sucked right out of them. My shadow flickered on the wall, watching. It *wanted* me to see what it had done.

I ran out of my apartment that day, sick and terrified. Stupid, really. How can you run from your own shadow? After Ralph, I stopped asking my shadow to do things. If I didn't ask for anything, maybe it couldn't do what it wanted. I thought that until Tommy Nelson's baby died. They said it was crib death, but I overheard one of the EMTs when they took little Joey away. The EMT sounded scared, and she said the baby's eyes looked like black marbles.

Joey died last night, and I phoned Mama this morning. She called me stupid. She called me foolish. Said I was messing with things I didn't understand. But she said she'd come. Mama had told me the truth when I was little. Your shadow is all that's ugly about you, it's all the bad thoughts you think when you're mad. Joey used to cry at night and wake me up. Ralph pissed on my bed once. Joey and Ralph made me angry, made me think terrible things, even for just a second. Things I would never do. My shadow remembered those things; it probably remembers a lot more.

I think it still needs me to get into this world, and if Mama can't fix this, I'll drive out to the old quarry off Route 23. The pond there is three hundred feet deep. I hope that far down there are no shadows.

The Sitting Room

The place he called the sitting room was cool and dry, with concrete walls and floor. The smell was pungent, but it never bothered him. It reminded him of the good work he'd done, how his collection had grown, and how each piece had changed over time.

A single chair was precisely positioned in the center of the room and allowed him to view the installation from a comfortable distance. He would sit for hours, pondering the changes that had taken place since his last visit. He allowed himself into the sitting room once a week; more than that and he feared it would lose its magic, its soothing nature. He longed for it constantly, though, and the need made it all the more satisfying when he finally went down and sat and looked.

The entrance to the old fallout shelter that would become his sanctuary had been sealed over when he'd bought the house a few years back. The realtor hadn't known it was there. He'd stumbled upon it while remodeling and immediately recognized its potential. It was isolated and quiet, a place made for private display. Before, he'd done his work where he'd found it, leaving little time to revel in the experience. It had to be quick, sudden, ugly—and these early endeavors were now lost to him. In the sitting room, he could linger over each new work, soaking it in for as long as he liked.

This was the second time he'd visited the room this week, but today was an exception. He had something new to display, and he wanted to get it on the wall as soon as possible. He'd dragged it down to the room in a burlap sack. It was big, and it would be difficult to mount, but he'd made the necessary preparations.

He stood in the center of the room, behind the chair, the new piece at his feet. He knew he'd made the right decision. The installation, while still beautiful, had begun to look incomplete. He always felt this way just before he added something new; a sense of the unfinished and a lack of purpose only new work would drive away.

He untied the burlap sack and grabbed hold of the piece. It left a red smear on the concrete as he dragged it toward the display wall. That bothered him. Colors went on the wall not on the floor.

The tools he needed were at the base of the installation: a four-pound sledgehammer, four stainless steel spikes, each six inches long, and a U-shaped bolt, eight inches long and four inches wide, sharpened on both ends. They were ordinary objects—things you could pick up at any Home Depot—augmented for his purposes. He had a sturdy block and tackle bolted to the ceiling that allowed him to raise a new work by its arms so it could be secured to the wall. He positioned his latest piece roughly three feet from the floor, then anchored the rope.

He started with the U-bolt. It provided the most stability. He carefully positioned it beneath the solar plexus with one hand and raised the sledge with the other. He struck a sharp, firm blow, and the twin spikes sank into the piece a good half-inch. Its eyes flew open at the shock and pain. This irritated him—it made the mounting more difficult when they squirmed. He much preferred they awaken during the viewing period; their movements added to the work.

The new piece opened its mouth, but both lungs had been perforated and nothing came out but a trickle of blood and a rattling gasp. He continued to hammer at the bolt until it had penetrated the flesh and bone and the wall behind it. The new piece thrashed the entire time, splattering him with its fluids. Finally, he'd had enough, and he smashed the sledgehammer into the side of its head. He heard a dull crunch and the new piece went limp. He frowned. Too hard. He hoped that wouldn't affect its aesthetic positioning on the wall or how it painted.

He did the feet next, hammering a steel spike through each instep. With the feet secured, he moved on to the wrists, one spike just below each hand. The new piece was secured to the wall, and already it had begun to paint, staining the concrete red behind it. In time, he'd make more holes to let other colors out—green, brown, more red.

He glanced along the wall where his previous works hung. The one next to the newest had begun to turn gray, and its painting had become muted. Farther along, the paintings grew more and more subdued, and the pieces themselves became withered and shrunken, completing their purpose. The new piece stood out from them, bold and exquisite, a shining monarch of color among its tired, gray subjects.

There was still much to do, but the chair beckoned him. He would sit for a while and watch the colors flow.

Two Legs

There had been no meat for too long. Mother's pups, now weaned off her milk, whined and yipped when she returned to the den, her jaws and belly empty. The squirrels and rabbits had gone, and nothing remained but parched desert and scorching heat. The smallest of her litter had already died, and its body had kept its brothers and sisters alive a little longer.

Mother lay down in the shade of the den. Her pups soon realized there would be no meat and curled up around her. She would sleep and conserve energy and then hunt in the cool of the night.

Sleep was almost upon her when a strange scent blew into her den on the acrid desert breeze. Mother breathed deep, and her keen nose built a picture in her mind. *Two Legs.* She raised her head, her ears swiveling, but heard nothing.

She had learned about the danger of the Two Legs from her dam. They kept meat selfishly behind barricades of wire and wood, and they could kill from a distance when unwary coyotes wandered too close to their dens.

Mother's mouth watered. Two Legs were dangerous, but beneath their strange scent, they were meat like everything else. She glanced at her pups and licked the nearest in her sleep. She had seen most of her own brothers and sisters die in the lean times, and she would do anything to keep that from happening to her own get.

She stood, the scent of the Two Legs stronger, closer. Mother was big, but Two Legs were larger than any coyote could safely kill alone. Taking prey of that size would require every ounce of strength and cunning she possessed, and success was still unlikely.

She looked at her pups again and made her decision.

Mother left the den and tracked the Two Legs over the hills and canyons, sticking to the shade to avoid the sun. She found her prey easily enough, walking alone along the bottom of a ravine. Mother licked her muzzle, excitement building. It was a female Two Legs, an adult, but a small one. It walked slowly, holding a small black box up to the sky that glinted in the sunlight. The Two Legs twisted about, as if confused, and it reeked of panic and fear.

Her prey distracted, a plan formed in Mother's mind. She had once come across a deer with a wounded leg. The beast had escaped a larger predator, perhaps a wolf or a mountain lion, but the wound had turned bad, and the deer had become too weak to run or even stand. It had been an easy kill, and she had gorged for weeks on the carcass.

Mother started down the side of the ravine, slinking low, using the shadows beneath the scrub brush to hide. Two Legs could see well, but they did not smell or hear like a coyote. She moved closer, her mouth hanging open, tongue lolling from hunger and dehydration. She would have to be quick.

The Two Legs had not seen her. It was preoccupied with the black box. It turned its back to her, and Mother sprang out from beneath a concealing bit of scrub, jaws agape. The Two Legs turned but too late. Mother locked her jaws around one of its legs, rich, tangy blood filling her mouth, and shook her head violently.

The Two Legs howled and beat at Mother's head, but she held on, shaking until she ripped a chunk of meat free, and then darted away. She ran up the side of the ravine, gobbling down the meat in one swallow. It would give her strength for what was to come.

When she reached the top of the ravine, she looked down. The Two Legs had fallen and dragged itself along the ravine floor, making the shrill noises of injured prey. Now she just had to wait and hope the other predators in the area would not find her prize.

*

A few days later, Mother led her pups to where the Two Legs had holed up in a small cave. Relieved, she smelled no other predators in the area. Her prey had nearly succumbed to its wound, and the bite on its leg had blackened with a spidery corona of infection.

The black box had fallen near the entrance of the cave, and it showed a curious image of smaller Two Legs. Mother realized they were pups, maybe her prey's own pups. She licked the black box. It tasted like sweat and blood. An odd compulsion seized her, and she picked up the strange object in her jaws and carried it over to the Two Legs. As Mother approached, it moaned softly and tried to crawl away, but it had little strength left. Mother dropped the box next to it and backed away, shooing her pups back with nips on their flanks.

The Two Legs quieted and picked up the box and stared at it for a time. Its breathing became labored and thick, and Mother smelled the change from life to death. The Two Legs released a long, rattling breath and lay still.

The pups yipped and howled around Mother, their desperate hunger and the scent of blood and meat driving them into a frenzy. Still, she kept them back and walked slowly up to the Two Legs and sniffed. It was dead and no danger. Mother yipped at her pups to come close, and they descended on the Two Legs.

Mother would eat when her pups had had their fill. She lay down in the shade near the cave entrance and listened to her get feasting and took contentment in the fading, alien smell of the Two Legs and the welcome and familiar smell of meat.

The Rarest Cut

Vincent cut into the meat, grimacing at the effort needed to saw through the stringy, pink flesh. He sliced off a portion, speared the chunk with his fork, and skated it through the fatty *au jus* pooling on his plate. He lifted the morsel to his nose and sniffed. The coppery tang told him the meat was quite rare, as he'd ordered it, but beneath that pleasant smell was a gamey odor that, of all things, reminded him of dirty laundry. He shrugged and popped the piece into his mouth and chewed.

The meat was firm, juicy, and the coppery smell was reflected in the taste. It reminded him of wild boar, an animal whose flesh he'd enjoyed in the past. He swallowed and frowned. The gaminess was stronger on his tongue than it had been beneath his nose. It lingered on his palate like an unwelcome guest.

The waiter, who stood behind him, stepped to the side of his table. "Is everything to your liking, sir?" He was tall, gaunt, and his skin had a yellow-orange tone that reminded Vincent of the antiseptic stuff surgeons swabbed on a patient before the incision.

Vincent cleared his throat, set his knife and fork on the table, and dabbed his lips with his napkin. "Well, I'm not a picky eater, and I consider my palate more refined than most, but this has an odd taste."

The waiter stared down at Vincent and nodded. His eyes were yellow like his skin. "Of course, sir," he said, his voice low, acquiescent. "If I may make a suggestion, I believe one should always sample new flesh twice before deciding if it is to one's liking. Wouldn't you agree?"

Vincent had traveled the world sampling the rarest and the strangest meats he could find. Some people collected coins or stamps; he collected unusual flavors and hard-to-obtain culinary experiences. He'd eaten Komodo dragon on the small island of Gili Motang, dined on black rhino in Cameroon, and he'd even traveled to Papua New Guinea only to find, to his immense disappointment, that the islanders' most infamous dish was more myth than reality.

Vincent glanced around the small, windowless restaurant, in which he was the only diner. The color red dominated the tiny space. Four tables with red tablecloths, soft crimson rugs, and magenta walls all made it feel as if he was eating some prized beast from the inside out. He'd first heard mention of the place from a Canadian couple as they dined on omelets from bald eagle eggs. Later, another connoisseur with whom he'd crossed paths from time to time mentioned the restaurant when he was in France eating elephant tongue. There had been others, too, gastronomic pioneers who shared his passion for unique culinary experiences. They had all assured him that here he would find everything he was looking for. When he'd finally found the nameless eatery in a part of town he'd never visited, he'd been unimpressed—until he'd viewed their menu and spoken with the chef.

"I think that's sound advice," he said to the waiter. "I mean, what are the chances I'll have the opportunity to eat something like this again?"

The waiter patted Vincent's arm with a spindly, long-nailed hand. "Exactly right, sir," he said, and then stepped behind Vincent's chair once more.

Vincent picked up his knife and fork and regarded the slab of rare meat on his plate. There were more bones than he liked; he could see their whitish outline just beneath the slightly translucent flesh. He cut off a small piece, forked it, and popped it into his mouth. It was better this time. The blood had congealed some, and the texture was firmer, which he enjoyed. He chewed and swallowed and then waited for the aftertaste. It wasn't overwhelming, but it was there, a dirty, musty flavor that canceled out any of the meat's better qualities.

"Nope," Vincent said and set down knife and fork again. "I just don't like this."

The waiter appeared at his side. "I understand, and I am so very sorry our cooks could not prepare this dish to your satisfaction."

Vincent held up his hands. "No, no. That's not the problem. It's cooked to perfection. I just don't like this meat."

The waiter nodded and rubbed his slightly pointed chin. "Perhaps you'd like to try another cut, then? In my experience meat from different parts of the same beast can have wildly different flavors."

"That is a fine idea." Vincent pulled the chair next to him out from under the table and propped his left leg on it. He rolled his pant leg up and over the expertly sutured stump at the end of his ankle, exposing plump white flesh. He picked up his fork, poked at the heavy calf muscle, and smiled up at the waiter. "Right about here should be good, I think."

The Last Scar

The morphine is starting to kick in when Sergeant Freeman raps his nightstick against my door. The key clicks in the lock, and the burly Marine steps into my room. "Stay where you are," he says, as if I could leave my bed without help and enough morphine to put an elephant in a coma.

Dr. Lanfield comes in behind Sergeant Freeman, a gaunt shadow in a white lab coat. "Hello, Scar. How are you feeling?"

"Not my name." I work the words through my uncooperative mouth. A grenade blast removed most of my right cheek three months ago. The scars have all but frozen the right side of my face.

"I'm sorry, *Kyle.*"

Usually, he'd go on calling me that bullshit name, but he wants something, and he thinks it'll be easier if he plays nice or pretends to. Fuck him.

"We have a mission for you."

The drugs have dulled the nerve-scraping agony along my spine enough to sit up. "No more. Finished." The word "mission" sent daggers into my brain, but I won't let him see that fear.

Dr. Lanfield sits in the plastic chair opposite my bed. Behind him, Sergeant Freeman looms. There was a time I might have fought them, and I know Freeman just aches for it, the sadistic fuck. But all I want now is to let the world slip away in a narcotic haze.

The doctor leans forward, feigning the compassionate physician. His usual bedside manner involves restraints and Freeman's nightstick. "I know you're hurting, and I know we haven't always seen eye-to-eye, but your ability has saved a lot of important lives."

I sneer at him. The shape of my mouth makes that one easy. "What about my life?"

"I'm sorry about all that, Kyle. Truly. How were we to know your gift would have these . . . these unforeseen consequences?"

I chuckle, even though it feels like my face might rip apart. I can heal any wound, no matter how bad, just like those guys in the comic books. Unlike those high-flying heroes, whose bodies heal perfectly every time, *my* gift—as Dr. Lanfield insists on calling it—leaves behind scars.

The scars are no big deal when it's a superficial cut or even the odd broken bone. They're an altogether different matter when you eat a full magazine from an AK-47 to save the Vice President from yet another assassin. I healed, but each bullet left behind scar tissue in my lungs, in my liver, in my muscles. They called me a hero, but I didn't feel like one when I jumped through the eighth-story window of the military hospital they keep me in, hoping the glass and the fall would kill me. It's not exactly comic book material when you wake up with most of your body held together with yet more scars and the knowledge maybe not even death can free you.

"No more."

Dr. Lanfield shakes his head and sighs. "I could let Sergeant Freeman persuade you, but with your rapidly deteriorating condition, that would not suit our purposes. So, I will make you an offer. Complete this mission, and it will be your last."

"Don't believe you." I hate the tiny spark of hope his words have kindled. He's lied to me before.

Dr. Lanfield shrugs. "Believe what you want. The mission requires only that you do what you do best: survive. Well, for a little while. Then it's over. The missions, the pain, all of it."

The tears surprise me. They stream down my battered face, a white flag signaling my compliance. I want what he is offering bad enough to do what he wants. He knows it, and his smile communicates that perfectly.

"One more." The desperation I hear in those two words hurts almost as much as speaking them.

*

My glider is remote piloted and flying low. They told me the enemy would not detect the aircraft until it was too late. Outside the canopy, a city appears on the horizon. It is the heart of the enemy's empire, five million people.

They've seen the glider, but they can't just destroy it. I'm too close. I could be carrying anything. Small arms fire erupts from the ground and bullets pierce the thin fuselage. I take a hit in the right leg, the left arm, and one bullet plows up through my left buttock, through my chest, and bursts from my neck in a shower of blood. The wounds heal almost instantly, leaving keloid trails in my skin. I have enough morphine in my system to keep the pain at bay for now.

The glider shakes as the bullet holes compromise its

aerodynamics, but I'm close. Buildings loom ahead, and the glider takes a sharp nosedive between them. People scatter as the ground rushes up to meet me. I brace for the impact, folding my body around the device.

Awful pressure.

Breaking glass.

Darkness.

*

The pain is a demon raking fire across my body when I come to. I would scream, but I can't draw enough air. A piece of rebar has punctured my chest and both lungs. My body has healed around it. Many of my bones have broken and then mended in gruesome, unnatural angles.

Voices drift through the shattered canopy. The enemy approaches.

Fighting through the agony, I inspect the device. It is intact. I toggle open the switch guard, and the button beneath flashes red. Dr. Lanfield promised this would be my last mission. He promised an end to the pain. For the first time he told me the truth. I don't think even I can come back from a thermonuclear blast at ground zero.

Frantic voices and then gunfire erupt outside the ruined glider. Bullets riddle my body, but I barely feel them. I will leave behind one last scar. I close my eyes and press the button.

Second Bite

Mr. Langley hobbled though the front door of my practice as the sun set, a tall, grim man with a face drawn by age and sickness. He leaned on a cane made from elephant tusk, and his breath wheezed in his lungs like branches scraping a windowpane. His coat was dirty, the vest beneath old and faded, and the silk handkerchief he pressed to his mouth stained with dried blood.

"Mr. Langley," I said. "You should not be out in this weather. The chill will only worsen your condition."

Langley waved away my warning. "Do you have it, Doctor Jansen?" His voice was hard as old iron despite his failing health.

I had dreaded this moment, and I was ashamed to say I had secretly hoped Mr. Langley might die before he could collect his order, no matter how desperately I needed his money.

"I have it."

"Show me." He shuffled to the glass counter where I keep examples of the dentures I carried. He was interested in teeth, but not those I sold to my patients.

I placed a teak box on the counter and removed the lid. Inside were a set of dentures, ivory white, the teeth perfectly shaped except for the canines. Seeing them made me queasy, summoning memories I had buried long ago.

Mr. Langley's eyes widened—they were a muddy green, the color of dying, rotting things—and his lips turned up in a smile. It was an ill-fitting expression on his haggard face. "Is it truly *him*?"

"Yes. All that remains." I replaced the lid and pulled the box away. "There is still the matter of payment, Mr. Langley."

He glowered at me but reached into his coat and placed a small, silken bag on the counter. I opened it and hundreds of perfect diamonds gleamed within. Langley owned mines in Africa and South America. His wealth was vast, and he needed those resources to convince me to part with the one thing of value I owned.

"There is enough to run your *little* practice for the next century should you wish," Mr. Langley glanced around at my shabby office. "You will install the teeth at once."

"There are risks," I said. "Your body is weak and—"

"You have your bloody money. Now do as I ask." He thumped his cane on the floor. This was not a man accustomed to questions or delays.

I pushed my reservations aside and stuffed the sack of diamonds into my coat. "This way."

*

Mr. Langley sat reclined in one of my dentist chairs, head back, mouth open. For a man of his age, his teeth were in surprisingly good condition.

"Mr. Langley, I must remove your natural teeth to install these dentures," I said. "There will be considerable pain, but with your age and health I cannot risk anesthetic."

He laughed, short and sharp. "My lungs are riddled with tumors eating me from the inside. I wake each morning and cough blood until I vomit, then spend my day wracked with agony I hardly thought possible. Pull the teeth, Doctor, and spare me your coddling."

I started with an incisor on the bottom jaw. The root of such a tooth is straight and cone shaped, making for an easy extraction. Mr. Langley did not flinch as my pliers crunched through the enamel nor did he move a muscle when I twisted the tooth from its socket. Methodically, I pulled the rest, and his face remained a stoic mask even as his mouth filled with blood.

When I finished, I pushed the dentures into his mouth. Generally, dentures must be custom fitted, the base formed to the contours of the patient's mouth. The blasphemous things I had made for Mr. Langley required no such preparation. They sealed instantly to his gums, soaking up the pooled blood.

He shuddered, and loosed a long, ragged breath. He did not draw another nor would he ever again. He wasn't dead, of course, he was something far worse. Mr. Langley's eyes remained open, and he blinked, once, twice, and sat up. His face had taken on an unusual pallor—bone white, the skin tighter, smoother, giving him an appearance of youth he did not possess. His eyes had gone from that revolting green to a brownish red, like old blood.

"I feel . . ." he said, holding his hands up to his face. The fingers were longer, thinner, his nails coming to a fine point. "Strong." He leapt from the chair with a whoop of joy, his body all but vibrating with energy.

I stepped back and undid the top two buttons of my shirt. He seemed to notice me again and turned, his new eyes filled with want, need, hunger.

"You know, Doctor, I did some research on you," he said. "Jansen is your mother's name."

I took another step back, toward the door. "Correct. My father's name carries certain . . . expectations."

"But such a strong name," Langley cooed, following me. "*Van Helsing*." My father's name rolled from his tongue like a curse.

I reached into my shirt and removed the golden crucifix. Langley recoiled, lips skinned back from his new teeth and long, pointed canines.

"Our business is it an end," I said, keeping the crucifix between us.

Langley's feral sneer became a smile. "Of course, Doctor." He gave me a wide berth and moved to the door. "I do hope you will not pursue your father's profession."

I laughed, but there was no mirth in it. "My father's profession bankrupted us. He died a laughing stock and a pauper. I have no wish to follow in his footsteps. Now leave."

Mr. Langley left my shop, his back straight, his gait quick and sure like a stalking beast. I held my father's crucifix and watched him disappear into the night, the bag of diamonds in my coat weighing on me like thirty pieces of silver.

Your Donation
Is Greatly Appreciated

A sudden wet, slapping sound at the front door sent a shudder running through Warren, and he lost all interest in the Astros game on the TV and the fresh can of Coors in his hand. He glanced over at his wife, Linda, eyes wide. "Didn't we just make a donation?"

She nodded, her eyes huge and damp. "Can't we just not answer the door?"

Warren shook his head. "No way. You know what happened to the Hendersons."

Linda grimaced. The patch of scorched earth across the street had once been the two-story home of their former neighbors, Rick and Gloria. Not even weeds grew there now.

The slapping returned, louder and more insistent.

Warren set his beer on the coffee table and ran a hand through his thinning hair. "I'm gonna get it," he said and rose from the couch.

Moving slowly, almost creeping, Warren made his way to the front door. He sucked in a deep breath and whispered, "It's for the greater good. It's for the greater good." He'd been telling himself that a lot lately. He grabbed the knob and pulled open the door.

"Mr. Daniels," the collection man said, its voice a liquid burble. "How are you this fine afternoon?"

"Uh, no complaints," Warren said, blinking and trying not to look directly at the collection man on his stoop.

Calling it a *man* at all was a stretch. Sure, it had a head, two limbs, and maybe even legs and feet beneath those black robes, but that's where the resemblance between the collection man and *Homo sapiens* ended. Its "face" was a ring of purple eyes orbiting a slick, sucker-like mouth, and a mass of short, writhing tentacles crowned its ovular head. The sleeves of the collections man's robes hung low, but not low enough to cover the nest of wormy appendages squirming beneath them.

"Excellent," the collection man said. The slimy hole in the center of its head crinkled up in a revolting yet reasonable facsimile of a smile. "My name is Mr. Q'lrqqsh. I'm here to collect your donation toward the continued success of our great president."

"Donation?" Warren said. "But I donated six months ago."

"You did, sir," the collection man said, its voice taking on a pleased gurgling. "And the President is most grateful, but, as you know, there is still much work to do."

"Is everything okay, honey?" Linda asked from the hall behind Warren. He squeezed over to allow her room in the doorway beside him.

"It's fine. Mr., uh, Klergish is here to collect our donation," Warren answered, trying to wrestle his tongue over the alien syllables.

"Mrs. Daniels," the collection man said. "Pleased to meet you." It raised an arm and offered the squirming mass at the end to Linda.

"Uck," Linda said, her mouth hanging open. She did not shake the collections man's "hand." Warren had made their donation last year. His wife had not encountered agents of the new administration before today, but the collection man didn't seem to take offense at Linda's reaction.

Warren glanced behind the government rep at the small cart resting on the walkway. A horde of buzzing flies rose above it, and its steel sides dripped with a telling rust color. A human foot and most of a leg stuck up over the rim.

"Okay, sure. I want to help, of course. How much do I need to give?" Warren said, tearing his eyes away from the cart.

The collection man reached beneath his robes and pulled out a stout book. The leather binding had a curious pinkish tone. A symbol—a star with an eye in its center—was stamped or maybe burned into the cover. "Let's have a look," it said and began turning the yellowed pages with a finger-tentacle. Its myriad eyes blinked over the pages, then it closed the book and shoved it beneath its robes again.

"Your previous donation was quite generous," the collection man said. "Let me be the first to say, *Ia Cthulhu Ftaghn!*"

Warren nodded. "Right, Kuthooloo Fatagan," he said, answering the campaign slogan with its appropriate response. "So how much?"

The collector's head-tentacles writhed. "A finger of your choice would be most appreciated," it said before leaning forward and opening its sucker. Inside the dripping maw awaited a forest of sharkish teeth.

"Honey, get a towel," Warren said. He closed his eyes,

and held out his left hand, pinky extended. He winced at the sharp spike of pain and the dull snap as the collections man's teeth sheared through the bone. The pain was bad, but the slimy mouth closing over his hand was far worse.

"Oh, my god!"

Warren's eyes shot open at the sound of Linda's voice. The first thing he saw was bright blood jetting from the stump of his finger. He fought down a wave of nausea, grabbed the towel from his stunned wife, and wrapped it around his hand.

"The President and I thank you for your contribution to the Great Vision. *Ia Cthulhu Ftaghn!*" said the collection man. "Good day." It oozed off the stoop, leaving a greasy stain in its wake.

Warren stepped back inside and shut the door with his elbow. "Glad that's over." He squeezed the bloody towel around his mangled hand.

Linda's face had gone pale as milk. She looked down at the prosthetic foot protruding from the bottom of her husband's right pant leg, remembering their last donation. "I wonder if we should have voted different."

"Well, consider the alternative," Warren said and winced. His finger had begun to throb. "I wasn't gonna vote for that fuckin' socialist."

Ditchers

"This will let me see who rings my doorbell?" Gary asked the SpyDoor technician, a beefy guy in a blue work shirt with the name Bob stenciled across the breast.

"That's right," Bob said, dusting the shiny new screen mounted next to Gary's front door. "Let me show you. Watch the monitor." Bob stepped outside, and a moment later the doorbell rang, a low rolling gong.

The screen flickered, then showed Gary's stoop, his manicured lawn, and the street behind it lined with stately brick Victorian homes. Bob waved at the camera, then stepped back inside. "Neat, huh?"

"Very. I'll finally see which of the little monsters is ringing my bell at all hours of the night."

"Oh, sure," Bob said and coughed. "You can also download the SpyDoor app and see the camera feed from your phone."

"Even better. You know, I might even file charges." Gary smiled at the possibilities.

"Charges? It's probably just doorbell ditchers." Bob frowned. "Kids being kids."

Gary frowned at the technician. "Oh, I'm sorry, Bob. You think I enjoy waking in the middle of the night so those—what did you call them?—*ditchers* can indulge their malicious urges?"

Bob put his hands up. "Hey, sorry. It's your system. Call them whatever you want."

"I'd call them criminals, deviants, little imps spawned

30

by awful adults and let loose to terrorize the neighborhood," Gary said. "Now, do I need to sign anything?"

"No. You're all set." Bob stood silent for a moment, then, "Go easy on the kids. We all did stupid—"

Gary reached around Bob and opened his door. "Have a good day."

*

Gary sat in his study and watched the fire, a glass of nice cabernet on the table beside him. His iPhone rested in his lap next to a legal pad and a pen. He couldn't help but grin. He was just so damn happy he'd finally bring his tormentors to justice. He'd made careful note of all the kids in the neighborhood so he would recognize their snot-smeared faces on sight. Tonight, he'd write down the names of each little shit to press the button. Then, tomorrow, he'd march over to their houses and demand justice from their useless parents. He'd threaten to call the cops. Threaten lawsuits. It would be glorious. If things went like the last two weeks, doorbell gonging into the wee hours of the night, he'd have a lot of names.

The doorbell rang—*gong*—and his cell phone buzzed in his lap. A message from SpyDoor read: *Your doorbell has detected a visitor.*

Excitement thrummed through him, and he stabbed his finger down on the message bubble. The screen showed a live feed of his stoop. He could see his welcome mat, the street beyond, and the bushes next to his entryway. Other than that, nothing.

"Damn," he said. "Not fast enough."

It didn't matter. There would be others.

31

He drained his wine glass and poured another. Instead of leaving the phone in his lap, he held it in his hand, a finger poised to jab the screen.

He didn't have to wait long. At five minutes past eleven, the doorbell gonged again, and the message appeared on his phone. He smashed the message bubble, and the feed of his stoop appeared again. He caught a flash of movement, something dark, and the bushes shook next to the entryway.

So close! They were fast. He'd give them that. Maybe they saw the SpyDoor technician and knew what it meant. They were cunning, like all low beasts.

"Next time," Gary mumbled.

He resumed his position, phone held close to his face, finger hovering above the screen.

Gong. The doorbell rang again, and he hit the SpyDoor message bubble. His stoop popped into view once more. This time, a short dark shape was visible on his welcome mat.

"Gotcha!" Gary said. "Now look up at the camera, you little fucker."

The head tilted, the face catching the dim shine from his porch light. Gary cried out and dropped his phone. It had not been a child's face on his screen, at least not a human child. The face was elongated, pushed forward, with a pointed nose and chin. Two glaring yellow eyes peering over its slit of a mouth, which spread to expose a forest of needle-like teeth.

Gary sat in his chair, shaking, silent, his stomach roiling. Minutes passed, and he took a long pull of wine. The sensible part of his mind reasserted control. "Okay, they saw the SpyDoor technician, and they knew I would see them tonight. So they put on masks to scare me."

Gong. The doorbell rang, and his phone buzzed on the floor.

He shook his head. No, no more. Not tonight.

Gong. His phone buzzed again. He refused to acknowledge it. Maybe they'd go away. But, of course, they never had before.

Gong, buzz. Gong, buzz. Gong, buzz.

Gary looked down at the phone between his feet. The doorbell rang twice more. He didn't want to see, but he knew he'd look anyway.

He picked up the phone and touched the message bubble. Horrid misshapen figures crowded his stoop, leering up into the camera. Glowing eyes and sharp teeth filled his screen. Beyond, terrible shapes dotted his lawn, and a line of little monsters wound into the dark street, all waiting for their turn.

Gary hurled his phone across the room, and it shattered against the wall. He covered his ears and squeezed his eyes tight.

Gong. Gong. Gong.

The Ruins by the Woods

The boy sat next to the ragged stone wall and wrapped his arms around his skinny knees. "I'm cold. When will my mom get here?"

Ruby pulled the hood around her face and settled beside him. "Soon. After dark."

The boy nodded. He moved close and grinned up at her. "You're warm."

Ruby smiled back and put her arm around him. He was seven or eight and small for his age. Finding a child eager to get into a stranger's car on the threadbare promise she'd drive him home had been lucky. Finding one who would believe his mother would meet him at a place outside the city had been luckier. He hadn't complained during the drive out to the ruins, and his stoic compliance made all this more difficult. He really was a sweet child. *I have no choice,* she thought. The truth didn't help. It never did.

The stones were cold against Ruby's back. They were always cold, even in the summer. The old, ruined cottage on the edge of the woods was little more than a jumble of crumbling masonry open to the elements, but the location was tradition. The cottage once belonged to an important ancestor, the first to make the offering.

It grew darker, and the first stars shone as bright pinpricks in the blue-gray curtain of the sky. The boy had grown quiet, his breathing slow and steady.

Ruby watched the sky and listened to the boy's soft

snores. Despite his warm body next to her, she shivered; the ruins grew colder as the night settled over them. Ruby tried to pull the hooded cloak tighter around her body. Ill-fitting and meant for a girl much smaller than she, the cloak was an old, moth-eaten thing, ragged and fraying, but it, too, was tradition.

The moon climbed into the sky, round and crimson, a great bloody eye staring down at the ruins below. Ruby grimaced in the moon-washed dark and licked her lips. A queasy surge of exhilaration hummed through her. Tonight would mark her third offering, and there was never a guarantee it would be accepted. If the beast refused, or if the boy escaped, she would stand in his stead. That had been Ruby's mother's fate, but her sacrifice had kept them safe, kept the beast from hunting her family for one more season. Now the cloak and the dreadful responsibility it carried had passed to Ruby, and the blood of the offerings would stain *her* hands.

A ragged, unearthly howl rose over the still ruins. The boy woke at her side, eyes wide. "What was that?" He moved closer, nearly climbing into her lap.

"Nothing to worry about." She stroked his pale blond hair. "She will be here soon."

He looked up at her and put his head against her shoulder. "Will you keep me safe?"

"Of course I will." She hugged him close. "You're a very special boy." He was a good boy, sweet, and she hated that his end must be so terrible.

Again, the savage howl splintered the night. It came from the woods and was louder this time, more persistent, much closer.

The boy pulled away from her. "I want to go," he squealed. "I want to go back to the car. My mom can find me there." He stood but Ruby pulled him down to her. She knew it would come to this; even such a docile offering would not go willingly.

"I'm sorry," she whispered. Ruby wrapped heavy arms around the boy, squeezing him close to her body. She climbed to her feet, carrying him with her. He struggled, but he could not break Ruby's embrace. He cried out, and she let him. It would bring the beast quicker, make the offering more pleasing. The boy quieted and his body fell limp in her grip—accepting prey before the inexorable predator.

Another howl, ear-splittingly close. The beast approached from the north, sliding through the ruins like a living shadow, a towering two-legged thing covered in black fur. Ruby heard its breath, deep and terrible, as it moved toward them. The thick gloom in the ruins obscured the beast's outline, but its yellow eyes shone through the dark, and its long jaws opened to reveal the ivory shards of its fangs. Black talons unfurled and reached for the boy.

She pushed him forward, into waiting claws. Rendered all but senseless, the boy made no sound and offered no resistance. Ruby did not turn away, as she knew her mother had. She watched and she listened as the beast consumed the offering. She viewed it as her penance for the part she played in the ancient ritual.

When it ended, and nothing remained but a red smear on the stone, the beast fixed her with its gaze. The copper scent of its kill and its dreadful outline struck her dumb, but the recognition in those jaundiced eyes was far worse.

Ruby closed her eyes and waited for the stinking heat of its breath on her skin just before those cruel fangs tore into her. Instead, the beast made a low rumbling noise, and when she opened her eyes, it was loping back toward the woods.

"Goodbye, Mother," she said into the dark and pulled the frayed red cloak tight around her shoulders. She fought against an almost manic giddiness bubbling inside her. In the days ahead, she would weep for the blood she'd spilled, but for now the Riding family was safe until the moon rose again, full and hungry.

An Incident on Dover Street

"What is it, Vince?" Dale said. "A wormhole or something?"

Vincent shook his head and glanced behind him. Some twenty of his neighbors stood in the middle of the street, staring at him expectantly. "How the hell should I know?" he said. "I'm not an astrophysicist."

Dale scratched the stubble on his chin, and casually swished an aluminum baseball bat through the air. "You're a scientist, though, right? Maybe you heard about something like this."

"Nope," Vincent said. "I'm as clueless as the rest of you."

"There's warm air coming through," Dale said, turning back to the hole. It gaped in the side of Pat Mavis' house, an eight-foot-diameter disc of perfect black. Vincent had thought it was some kind of trick, a well-executed optical illusion until Dale had thrown an empty beer can at it—into it. Pat and his wife Judy were out of town or god knows what might have happened to them.

Dale was right; Vincent could feel a warmish breeze, and the humid air clashed with the dry, crisp California autumn. "Dale, the cops will be here soon. Let them handle this," he said. A number of the residents of Dover Street already had cell phones in hand.

"Come on, Vince," Dale said. "Aren't you a little interested in a goddamn hole in space and time or whatever?"

"I'm not that kind of scientist, Dale." He sounded irritated but he was scared shitless, really. The noise that had preceded the appearance of the hole was like nothing he'd ever heard, a massive tearing, scraping sound that had filled the world and shaken his house like a small earthquake.

The sound had pulled everyone out of their houses. Only Dale Oslow, the street's resident tough guy, had been brave enough to get close to it, though. Vincent stood in the no man's land between Dale and the sidewalk, on the edge of the lawn, closer than anyone but Dale; that made him feel a little brave and a little stupid.

"Something's moving in there," Dale said and stepped toward the hole.

"Then get the fuck away from it," Vincent said, a creeping sensation worming into his gut. A shape *had* appeared, a wavering, indistinct figure standing out against the nebulous darkness. The shape grew more distinct, and it reminded Vincent of something he should recognize. When it came out of the hole, he nearly pissed himself.

"Is that a giant chicken?" Dale said, eyes wide.

Vincent wanted to tell his neighbor that the ten-foot-long, feathered, bipedal creature with hooked, narrow jaws filled with backward curving fangs and a pair of gutting hooks on its bird-like feet was not a giant chicken. He knew this because he was actually *that* kind of scientist, a paleontologist, but he couldn't get his mouth and tongue to work. He managed one word.

"*Deinonychus*," Vincent said. He *wanted* to shout that a goddamn *raptor*—one of the infamous stars of *Jurassic*

Park—had strolled out of space and time and now stood in all its feathered glory on their quiet, suburban street.

"I'm gonna fucking brain that thing before it hurts somebody," Dale said and strode forward, raising his baseball bat.

The dinosaur's wedge-shaped head whirled around, orienting on the movement. Its huge, forward-set eyes fixed on Dale, and it opened its jaws, loosed a hissing screech, and sprang.

The *Deinonychus* covered the ten feet between the hole and Dale in a single leap, a blur of feathers and fangs, its legs pulled close to its body so those merciless talons would hit first. Vincent heard the hollow metallic thud of the aluminum baseball bat connecting, but the dinosaur still knocked Dale flat.

Vincent stumbled back. The dinosaur raked Dale's body like a rooster scratching for grubs, opening up gaping wounds. Dale's intestines spooled out of his savaged belly like slippery, pink eels.

The residents of Dover Street ran in all directions, screaming. Vincent nearly ran too, but he was captivated by the creature eating his neighbor. Elated thoughts ran through his head. *They do have feathers! They do have binocular vision! They ARE birds!*

The *Deinonychus* pushed its head down and through Dale's flailing arms, clamping its jaws on either side of his skull. His screams grew muffled, and then abruptly stopped when the raptor jerked its head up, ripping away most of Dale's face in a single glistening flap of meat.

The street had fallen silent, but a frenzied thought burst through Vincent's head like a klaxon alarm. *Pack hunters!* More shapes moved in the hole, and he counted seven before he turned and ran.

His world dissolved into just three things: the acrid burning in his lungs, the hammering thunder of his heart, and a sound no other human beings had ever heard—the clicking of dinosaur talons on asphalt.

Small Evil

I appear in the middle of a crudely drawn pentagram, the energy of a weak containment spell spilling over my skin like the legs of a thousand tiny spiders. Beyond my mystical prison stand five humans in a windowless basement apartment. They wear what look suspiciously like bathrobes dyed black, and not one of them is a day over twenty-five.

I don't have time for what is clearly amateur hour. I was in the middle of a torture session with my five o'clock, and, if these motherfuckers put me behind, Baal is gonna have my ass.

I need to get this show on the road. "Which of you assholes summoned me?"

One of the humans lowers the hood of his robe with a flourish, like Obi-Wan Fucking Kenobi or something, revealing an angular and surprisingly handsome face. "Harken to me, demon. I am Arthur Edgerton, and—"

"Can we not do the whole Dungeons and Dragons rigmarole, Arty?" I say. "Cut to the chase."

"Uh, what?" Arty says, startled. Maybe he didn't expect me to speak. He glances back at his compadres, four other pasty white dudes, but they're clueless.

"Look, man, somehow you idiots pulled off a summoning ritual," I say. "So, you know, bravo for that shit, but I got things to do. What do you want?"

Arty regains his composure, clears his throat, and straightens his shoulders. "I command you, demon, to do my bidding."

He called me "demon" again, and I realize Arty doesn't know my true name. Only a weak containment spell prevents me from ripping his guts out through his asshole. Well, okay then. This might be fun.

"Sure thing, Arty. How can I do your bidding?"

Arty brightens. He thinks he's in charge now. "Demon, I wish you to destroy my enemies, to visit upon them incalculable suffering, to—"

"Can you just give me a name or something?"

"Oh, yeah, sure." He reaches into his bathrobe, pulls out a piece of paper, and holds it up. It's a picture of a young woman with dark hair. It looks like a profile pic.

"What's her name, Arty?"

"Jessica Monroe," he says, and I feel a little tremor in the air. Demons are attuned to human evil. We can smell it like a ripe fart in an elevator. Ol' Arty really hates Jessica and wears his bruised ego like a fucking halo.

"What'd she do to you, Arty?" I ask, intrigued by this wannabe Satanist's hate-on for young Jessica.

"She insulted me. Publicly," he says and frowns. His lips tremble like he might cry.

"You send her a bunch of dick pics or something?"

"No!" he says and recoils. Apparently snapping a photo of his junk is over the line for Arty, while summoning the minions of hell is not. "She posted one of the emails I sent her."

I sigh. "What was in that email, Arty?"

"Nothing. I just . . . like her, and she told me to stop emailing her, and . . . I was just being nice!"

"Uh-huh. So, you want to me do what? Kill her? Possess her?"

His eyes light up. "You could possess her?" Behind him, his cadre of fellow dumbshits nod and grin.

"Yeah, I could do that, Arty," I say. "But you gotta drop this containment spell." It's true; I can possess humans, but only ones who open themselves up to it. I seriously doubt Jessica Monroe has been dabbling in the dark arts, but I know five motherfuckers who have.

"Oh," he says, and his eyes narrow. "Wait a second." He runs over to a bookshelf and grabs a paperback with a black cover and a bunch of spidery symbols on it. I recognize it immediately. It's the *Simon Necronomicon*, a book of "spells" you can purchase at Barnes & Noble for $8.99. I don't know where Arty learned how to do an honest-to-god summoning and containment ritual, but it sure as fuck wasn't from the *Simon Necronomicon*.

He comes back, stands before me, and flips through the pages of his "spell book." He finds what he's looking for and begins to read aloud. I suppress a big shit-eating grin and try to look scared and pissed off as he finishes his "demon control" spell.

"There," Arty says. "Now it can't hurt us."

"Hey, man, are you sure," one of Arty's fellow Satanists says. "That thing looks—"

Arty whirls and points at his acolyte. "Shut up, Dave. I got this." He turns back to me. "Now, demon, you are under my power."

"Yes, Master," I say with just the right amount of angry subservience. "Free me and I will serve you."

"Fantastic," Arty says and smudges one of the lines on the pentagram with his foot. I feel the containment spell wink out.

"Fantastic, indeed," I say. "Let's go to work."

*

Being in Arty's body is not an unpleasant experience. He works out, and I didn't have to expend much demonic mojo to get him moving at a good clip. I lick the blood off Arty's fingers and look down at the four corpses I helped him create. The idiots didn't have any real weapons, but the butcher knife I found in the kitchen did the trick.

Arty's horror as he watched himself murder his friends was delectable, but I couldn't take my time like I normally would have. Things to do, souls to torture. Of course, all these assholes are gonna end up in hell, so I have eternity to get intimately acquainted.

I reach down and pick up Jessica Monroe's picture. I hold it up so Arty can see it and put the blade of the butcher's knife against our throat. I draw the knife across Arty's jugular, reveling in his panicked terror as the blood leaves his body in throbbing jets.

"Jessica," I say. "This one's on me."

Time Waits for One Man

"Okay, so you're immortal?" Nadine set her iPhone on the table and pressed record.

"I won't register on that," said the man seated across from her. He was tall and thin, with a sharp nose, a wide, clear brow, and eyes so brown they were almost black. She wouldn't call him handsome in the classic sense, but there was an indefinable allure.

"Oh, why not?" Nadine said.

"I am not entirely sure, but it seems to be part of my...condition. Technology newer than a few centuries doesn't work particularly well around me."

Nadine put her phone away and pulled a legal pad and a pen from her bag. "Okay, we'll do this the old-fashioned way. Start from the top. You're immortal."

The man sat back and sipped his wine. "It is more accurate to say I cannot die."

"How do you know that?"

"You witnessed that automobile strike me, and yet here we sit."

Nadine would never forget the incident. She'd come out of the *Seattle Times* building and saw a man crossing the street. He didn't see the Lincoln Navigator racing to beat the yellow light. She'd called out a warning, but too late. The SUV plowed into the man and threw him thirty feet, where he landed in a heap of twisted limbs. People raced over to help, but before anyone reached him, the man climbed to his feet and sprinted away. She'd searched for him for a month.

When she'd tracked him to one of the many tent cities in Seattle, he agreed to talk to her for a meal.

She sipped her martini. "Well, I saw *something*. That's why I tracked you down."

"That vehicle shattered my spine, destroyed multiple internal organs, and fractured both arms and one leg. You saw that."

She shuddered. "I won't lie. I thought you were dead until you got up and ran off. How is that possible?"

"I do not remain injured, even fatally, for long." He took another pull from his wine glass, and his eyes became cloudy, far away. "This is quite good, but nothing compares to a Constantinople sweet red from around 1150."

"Wine you had nine hundred years ago, huh?"

He laughed. "I know; it is hard to believe."

"Okay, let's get back on track. You survived this car accident, but that kind of thing happens. It's freakish, but it happens. So why would I believe you can't die?"

He frowned. "You're a reporter; I'm sure you found out what happened to the driver of that car."

She swallowed. "I tried to interview him, yes."

"And why didn't you?"

"He's dead. Two weeks ago, a semi-truck ran him over and dragged him nearly two miles."

The man's frown deepened. "I didn't want that to happen. It has been some time since I lived in a city, and I am forgetful of its dangers. That man paid for my mistake, but that's how this works."

"How what works?"

"Look at this." He parted his black hair—remarkably clean for a man living in a tent on the street—exposing his forehead. There was a scar there. No, a brand, a letter maybe, but from a language she'd never seen.

"I don't understand. What is that?"

"Angelic script. It's the reason I'm still alive, and the reason that poor man who hit me is dead."

Nadine had heard a lot of bullshit stories in her ten years as a reporter, but there was a sincerity here, an apathy toward her opinion of the situation that gave her pause. Still, a man who miraculously survived what should have been a fatal injury made a decent story unto itself.

"May I have another glass?" he asked.

Nadine signaled the waiter. "Another glass of the red, please." When the waiter left, she said, "Okay, if you're immortal, why are you living on the street? Why aren't you fabulously wealthy?"

"A good question," he said. "The truth is simple. I am cursed to wander, to never settle anywhere for long. One cannot build an empire of wealth with such a transient nature."

It was plausible if you bought the rest of his story. Of course, the rest of his story could be proved easily. Nadine decided to call his bluff. "Okay, listen, I carry a gun in my purse. Let's go somewhere quiet and you can demonstrate your immortality."

He recoiled. "Have you not been listening? If you shoot me, you'll see I'm telling the truth, but then you will pay, horribly."

"Because someone will shoot me?"

"Yes, or worse. Anyone who harms me has the same harm visited upon them sevenfold."

That reminded Nadine of something, but she couldn't put her finger on it. "Then we don't have much to go on."

"There are other ways I can convince you," he said, his eyes suddenly eager.

"Yeah, how's that?"

He leaned over the table. "Let me tell you my story. You can write it down, make a book out of it. A very long book."

That intrigued her. Even if he was full of shit, it might make an interesting story.

The waiter brought the wine, and the man took a sip and nodded approvingly. "All I want in return is more of this." He waved his hand at the restaurant around them. "Wine, good food, company, and you get a story no one has ever heard."

"Okay, here's what I'll do. We'll meet three more times, and you can have all the wine and food you want on my dime. If, after those three meetings, you haven't provided me with anything I can believe or use for a story, we part ways. Deal?"

"Deal." He extended his hand, long-fingered and strong. She shook it.

"Okay, first things first. What do I call you?"

He smiled again, but there was sorrow in his eyes, old and powerful. "You may call me Mr. Adamson."

49

Simulacra

Ice and a snow weren't the best material for the task, but Jason didn't have much else to work with. He could cobble something together from the shattered concrete and rubble around the stadium, but it seemed like so much work, and he was so damned tired. Ice and snow would do.

He used an icicle from the underside of the bleachers as the spine for his first creation, anchoring it to the concrete with packed snow. He clumped and compacted more snow around it until he had a rough, human-shaped form about four feet tall. From his pocket, Jason took the sapphires he'd found in the burnt-out wreck of a jewelry store and pushed them into the ice person's head.

"Julie," he said. Her blue eyes had gleamed like sapphires when he proposed, like a sky he hardly remembered.

Julie sat in a shallow bowl of concrete that looked down on a patch of mud and weeds that might have been a football field before the bombs fell. Once attached to a high school, the stadium had somehow survived the destruction of the school and most of the town around it. Its bleachers were the kind that made your ass sore ten minutes after you sat down, and it looked like they might hold a couple hundred people. He only needed three seats.

The sun shone feebly through a thick cover of yellow

clouds, offering only a dim and painful reminder of warmth. He'd looked upon the same cancerous sky for two wretched years of endless winter and hunger.

Jason returned to the work; it would be dark soon, and he wanted to finish in what little daylight remained. He broke another icicle free, smaller this time, and set it next to Julie. He piled snow around it, his breath steaming over the form taking shape. He imagined breathing what little of his life remained into the stiff, frozen figure. A ridiculous notion, but he found some satisfaction in the idea it might contain some piece of him, some molecule of his essence.

The second ice person was tiny, child-sized. He fumbled at the pocket of his coat for the last piece he needed. The snow had soaked his woolen gloves, and his fingers felt like pieces of wood. *Frostbite.* He pulled out a picture he'd cut from a magazine, a smiling baby boy, maybe six months old, on a blanket with his parents. They sat on a manicured lawn in a world that no longer existed.

"I know you always liked the name Robert." He recalled Julie with her hands cradling her round belly, her face alight with joy and irritation. He let the tears come, let them freeze on his face like strings of diamonds. "But I'm a junior, and I always thought it'd be cool for our son to be a third, like royalty. I hope you can forgive me."

He folded up the picture of the baby and its parents and pushed it into the second ice-person's chest. "Jason," he said, "the Third."

*

The sun sank lower in the sky and the temperature dropped. Nuclear winter was a bitch, and he doubted the temperature had risen above freezing since he left San Diego two years ago. He shivered hard, and the cold reached through his coats with jagged fingers, squeezing the warmth from his core. Usually, by this late in the day, he'd huddle up next to a fire made with whatever burnable trash he could find. He was done with that. The world had died, succumbed to cold and dread. What point was there to holding off the inevitable any longer?

Jason released a long, shaking breath and sat down next to his family. The snow had collected in tall mounds between the concrete seats, and he pulled it over himself like a frigid, gray blanket. He covered his lap, lay back, and piled more snow on his chest, letting the cold seep into him. His shivers became a wracking whole-body thing, but that would pass.

He knew his wife and son beside him were only simulacra. Their bones lay in the mass grave that used to be Los Angeles, their ashes mingled with the incinerated remains of countless millions. These bodies, shaped from the bitter remains of a dead world, were a statement of life, however fleeting. They brought him some comfort, though *closure* might be a better word.

He was not religious, and he had no delusions about seeing his family beyond the darkness. It was enough that no one would have to watch the sun rise over an empty world again.

He stopped shivering. The violent quaking of his chilled body gave way to languid warmth that started at his head and flowed down his limbs. Jason's eyelids grew heavy, and before long he couldn't move his arms and legs. He turned his head back to a sulfurous yellow glow on the horizon.

He watched the sun set one last time and welcomed the darkness like an old friend, like family.

Part II
Midnight

Reunion

"Does it hurt them, Daddy?" Evelyn asked. Her voice, whisper-soft and gurgling, reminded Jeremiah of the dark and the deep, of the lightless realm where the masters lived.

Jeremiah looked away from the ceremony up the beach and smiled down at his five-year-old daughter. Her upturned face bore the Dreamer's mark: round, goggling eyes; wide, flat lips; and the almost invisible gill slits on either side of her neck. She was beautiful, but the mark had become more pronounced of late. Jeremiah home-schooled her now to keep from frightening the newcomers, residents not of the old families who settled Almhearst three hundred years ago.

"It does hurt them," he said and took Evelyn's tiny hand in his, caressing the translucent membrane between her thumb and forefinger. "But only for a moment."

Evelyn frowned and pointed up the beach. "Mr. Hendricks gave me candy. He's nice."

Jeremiah glanced back at the ceremony. The villagers of Almhearst stood near a massive pit in the sand, their figures looming and distorted against the bonfire behind them. Chief Davies and Deputy Richards each held one of Sylvester Hendricks' arms. They were large men, and they kept the owner of the Almhearst Dime & Drug immobile between them. Shirtless, his naked torso fish-belly pale, Mr. Hendricks bawled and moaned. Normally, Sylvester was quite an articulate man, but his powers of speech had abandoned him after he'd seen the fate of the other newcomers.

"He is . . . *was* nice, honey," Jeremiah said.

Gunther Almhearst, one of the village elders, approached Mr. Hendricks, the long whale-bone knife in hand. Gunther would soon return to the sea, and his blessed transformation was visible even from where Jeremiah stood a hundred yards from the ceremony. This was the first time Sylvester Hendricks—or any newcomer—had met Gunther. The shopkeeper's howls became high-pitched and terrified when he got a good look at the village elder's face. Gunther knew his business and did not prolong the inevitable. He plunged the knife into Mr. Hendricks' chest below the breastbone and ripped the blade down through the flesh beneath it. Mr. Hendricks' screams turned to hoarse grunts as his entrails unspooled into the pit before him. Chief Davies and Deputy Richards held him up, letting the viscera unwind, and then let his limp body fall. The soft, contented piping of the growing shoggoth drifted up from the hole.

Jeremiah turned back to his daughter. Her fish-like mouth gaped open, exposing the tiny needly barbs behind her human teeth. She was breathing heavily, and tears clouded her glassy, protuberant eyes. "Why did Mr. Almhearst hurt Mr. Hendricks?"

Jeremiah squeezed his daughter's hand. "I know it's hard to understand, honey, but tonight is a special night. We give the blood of the newcomers to create the vessel." Behind them, a woman screamed. Henrietta Bright,

Evelyn's teacher, was next. "The vessel—the holy shoggoth made from the flesh of the newcomers —summons the masters to the shore. Can you hear it?"

The piping from the pit grew louder as Mrs. Bright's frenzied shrieks came to a sharp and sudden end. The shoggoth's call was musical and soothing.

"I like that sound," Evelyn said, wiping her eyes. She offered her father a shy smile. "It's pretty."

"For my pretty girl," he said, bending down to take his daughter's face in his hands. He kissed her broad forehead. Near-invisible scales rasped against his lips. "And it carries deep into the ocean so the masters can hear."

"When will they come?" Evelyn asked.

Jeremiah turned back to the ceremony. The last of the sacrifices had been made, and the villagers gathered around the pit. They chanted now, low and burbling. The shoggoth responded to the cadence of the chant, and its piping grew louder, rhythmic and eager.

"Soon, honey," Jeremiah whispered. He could feel the energy gathering, and the pounding of the surf seemed to echo in the villagers' chanting. The shoggoth rose from the pit, a towering monolith of squirming flesh. Its bulbous surface was pocked with the slack, staring faces of the newcomers and a myriad of less-recognizable appendages, orifices, and sensory organs. Its flute-like call reached a piercing crescendo, a penetrating wail the filled Jeremiah with an unnamable longing.

"Daddy!" Evelyn cried. "Look at the sea."

Jeremiah turned to see the inky water of the Atlantic shining with a soft green glow. It grew in intensity, the shimmer made up of hundreds of individual lights rising toward the surface like a field of emerald stars.

The first of the masters flopped from the water a dozen yards from where Jeremiah and Evelyn stood, its black scales glistening in the moonlight, the bioluminescent patches along its back glowing a pale verdigris. It stood on two legs that bent forward at the knees and opened its fanged maw to breathe in a gulp of night air. The gills along its neck shuddered and then closed in the alien atmosphere.

The creature advanced up the beach, shambling and hopping toward Jeremiah. He saw the glint of gold beneath the barbels on its chin. The heart-shaped locket was grimed over but still visible hanging from its slender chain. Jeremiah's breath caught in his throat, but Evelyn made the connection first.

"Mommy!"

When the Lights Go On

We don't turn on the lights in Moore, Idaho.

The men from the plant said we're imagining things. They accused us of mass hysteria because the light they provide comes from the same power that destroyed Nagasaki and Hiroshima.

I've been to Arco, a few miles north of us. They were the first, and they don't turn on their lights either. They use fireplaces and gas lanterns too, like it's 1855 and not a hundred years later. Of course, the government and the men from the plant don't believe Arco either. They don't believe the energy coursing through the wires, shining around us, *into* us, does what we say it does.

We'll have to show them.

Moore's entire population, all one hundred and fifty people, have gathered inside the pristine white walls of the church. They are silent, even the children sit quiet and still next to their parents. Hope and light have gone out of Moore. Only darkness and fear remain.

A gas lantern burns on Pastor Lewis' podium, the only light in the church. Strings of bulbs hang from the ceiling overhead, but we won't turn them on until we have to. It doesn't take long once we switch on the lights.

There is a knock on the church doors, and Pastor Lewis nods to me. "Sheriff, if you would."

I walk to the wide double doors and open them. Outside stand two men in black suits and two more in those crazy space suits the men at the plant wear. The black suits are here in case we're crazy; the space suits in case we're not.

"Sheriff Norris?" one of the black-suited men says, his smile so bright it, too, might be powered by a nuclear reactor.

"That's me."

"I'm Agent Sims; this is Agent Daniels." He nods to the other black suit. "We've brought the experts you requested."

"Good, come on in."

The four men step inside the church and everyone cranes their necks to get a look.

"Welcome, gentlemen," Pastor Lewis says. "We appreciate you making the trip."

Agent Sims points to the space suits. "These men will detect any anomalies with the power you're getting from the reactor. We'd like to put your fears to rest."

"That's all we're asking," I say.

Agent Sims frowns. "Kind of dark in here. Can we turn on the lights?"

The fear in the room is immediate. We all know what must come next. We don't want it this way, but what options were left to us? Only when we stopped using the lights, stopped participating in their experiment, did the men from the plant agree to come and see. Now there's no turning back.

Pastor Lewis nods at me again, and I move to the light switch near the door.

"Well?" Agent Sims says.

"Look, Mister," I say. "I know you think we're a bunch of yokels afraid of your new technology. That's not it.

There's something *wrong* with the power that comes from that plant."

Agent Daniels speaks for the first time. "There's nothing *wrong* with science and progress."

"Not usually," I concede then turn to address the town. "Everyone, move away from the wall. Just like we practiced."

People move to the west side of the church beneath the big windows there, leaving the east wall a blank, white canvas. We've done this a couple of times, and I know where the light will hit.

Agent Sims watches all this with a smirk. He's amused. That won't last.

"Agent Sims," I tell him. "I don't want anyone to get hurt. When I turn on the lights, you need to be ready."

His eyes narrow. "Ready for what, Sheriff?"

"To run."

I flick the switch.

The lights overhead flare to life, and the town's shadows appear on the east wall. They are static, unmoving, and too dark, as if the light has burned them into the stucco. I once saw a picture of Hiroshima after the bomb, of shadows scorched into the sidewalks and sides of buildings. The shadows in the church are like that. At first.

"I don't understand." Agent Sims is looking at me, not at the wall.

"What the fuck?" The other fed, Agent Daniels, has seen them. The shadows that are not shadows. They flicker and writhe in the bright glow of nuclear power. No one in the church has moved.

"It's a trick." Agent Sims' voice shakes. He's seen them too. "What are you people playing at here?"

"You've seen. Now go. Please." They don't listen, and I know what happens now. They have to be convinced.

The shadows in Hiroshima were imprints, created and then wiped out in the blast. In Moore and in Arco, the energy suffuses our bodies and souls in a slow trickle. It has done us no visible harm, but our shadows are alive and hungry.

One of the men in space suits cries out. He was too close to the wall. Slithering tendrils of darkness coil around his body and pull. He comes apart in a spray of blood, adding crimson to the roiling black.

Agent Daniels pulls his pistol and gets off two shots, thunderously loud inside the church. The shadows grab him too, hoist him aloft, and tear him to pieces.

Agent Sims runs, dragging the second space suit behind him. I flick the switch as the men from the plant head for the door, and for a heartbeat too long the shadows remain. I am seized with the terrible notion they no longer need the lights, but the black shapes tumbling and writhing on the wall fade as darkness fills the church.

Someone weeps, but there are no cries of disgust or outrage over the two dead men. We've seen worse.

Pastor Lewis breaks the silence after a few moments. "Will they believe us now?"

I lean against the wall, suddenly exhausted. "I hope to god they do. The lights go on in Butte City next week."

62

The Thing That Came with the Storm

I've burned all the furniture and every scrap of paper in the house. I even ripped up the hardwood floors and pulled the studs out of the walls. I might have a few more days, maybe a week before there's nothing left for the fire. After that, the cold comes in, and *it* comes too.

I saw it the first day after the storm. The power went down, and the streets became rivers of snow and ice. It floated down Sinclair Street in the bright winter sun, dragging the remains of Mrs. Gilliam. It had eaten parts of her, and as I watched, frozen with horror, from my front window, it tore a chunk from her thigh and pushed the gobbet of flesh into its mouth.

It sensed me and turned in my direction, an emaciated skeleton clad in bone-white flesh, its face all eyes and teeth, its tattered lips wrenched up in a graveyard smile. It rushed my house and then stopped, as if held at bay by some invisible barrier. It lingered a few moments at the edge of my sidewalk, and then returned to Mrs. Gilliam's corpse. I watched as it ate her, a small, shy woman who had loved crosswords and coffee on her porch. I have never been so terrified, but I needed to see it leave, and it did, eventually.

It appeared again the next day. I was thinking about going for help, despite temperatures hovering at negative seventy degrees. I was about to walk out my door when it floated down the street. It held the top half of Mr.

Fiddler in one icy claw, his legs dangling from its mouth. It was so much bigger, a towering specter of madness and hunger. Its body was still wasted, though, its bones poking tents in its ashen skin.

It came up to the house, closer this time, within ten feet of my front door before it turned back and floated away. The warmth had stopped it. I know that now. My pitiful fire is a ward against it.

Now I keep the fire high and huddle next to the fireplace in my front room. The thermal underwear, two sweaters, and my parka barely ward off the cold. I sit close enough to the fire that it should be uncomfortable, but its heat is diminished, sucked away by the unnatural chill. I have a bottle of lighter fluid, but I'm saving it for a last kiss of warmth before it takes me.

I don't know what it is, but you don't live in Mackinaw City without hearing a few legends and myths about the cold. This land belongs to the Chippewa, and they have a casino across the bridge in St. Ignace. I gamble there sometimes, and whenever we have a bad winter, the folks at the casino get a little edgy, a little different. It's like they're afraid of the cold. Now I know why.

I haven't seen it in a few days, and that worries me. Am I alone or are there others huddled in their homes around a fire, waiting for the cold to end? Have they gone out like I tried to do, away from the protection of their hearths? I remember how much bigger it was last time I saw it, and how it still ate, as if nothing could fill it.

Night has fallen, and I put another piece of flooring on the fire. The fumes from the burning varnish choke me, but it's better than the cold.

There is no wind, no birds, no insects, just the dead silence of an icy tomb. I inch closer to the fire and look out my window. Across the street, the dark shapes of houses thrust up like jagged teeth in the moonlight. Then I see a shape I mistake for a tree, until it moves.

It floats toward my house, fifty feet tall, blotting out the stars with its immensity. Its face is a moon of white death and black teeth.

I know my fire won't hold it back. It is too strong, too cold. I cast around for something to build my fire higher, but there is nothing. The creature fills my window, and its chill rips the breath from my lungs.

I fall to my knees, watching my fire dwindle. The foundations of my house groan and the window shatters. The fire is only coals now, and I reach for the bottle of lighter fluid and squeeze a stream of hissing liquid into the blaze. The burst of warmth and flame throws heat across my body, and the creature shrieks and pulls away from the window.

I can't keep the fire high unless I find something else to burn, something bigger.

I stand and squirt lighter fluid over the wall next to the fireplace, then squeeze a line on the floor, and then into the fire itself. The fluid catches, and a blazing dagger jumps from the floor to the wall. The plaster and insulation catch, a sheet of fire that bathes the room in blessed warmth.

The ceiling catches next, and the thing retreats further, smashing through a house across the street. Flames soon engulf the front room, and I run outside and watch my house go up. I use the last of my lighter fluid to spray the fence between my house and the neighbor's. The fence catches, then the house, and the one next to it.

I move with the growing fire, as close as I dare, inching toward the bridge in the distance.

Maybe I can get to the casino and someone there will know what to do. I glance back, and the creature floats in the distance, hanging in the night sky like an awful constellation. It howls its fury as the houses burn. Maybe the fire will take me. Maybe that isn't so bad.

Far Shores and Ancient Graves

"Dr. Livingstone, I presume." Grace smiled, hoping the stuffy-looking British archaeologist had a sense of humor.

He appeared tired, fuzzy around the edges, and his face was pale and drawn. Still, he returned the smile. "This may surprise you, but I've heard that one before." He stepped away from a collection of skeletal remains on an examination table and stuck out his hand. She shook it.

"My apologies." Grace laughed. "Now, tell me, why request a forensic anthropologist from the other side of the pond without telling her exactly why?"

"I'm sorry about that, but we have a, well, sensitive situation, and I thought your work in Salem might lend you special insight."

The secrecy around this whole thing began to make sense. "The witch trial graves. You know my theories there aren't exactly conventional."

"Neither are these remains."

*

Halfthor stood near *Draken's* bow and pointed his sword at the shore. "Look brother; they come to greet us."

Aksel grinned and adjusted the mail shirt on his shoulders. Behind him his small crew made final adjustments to armor and weapons. "Like those fools last week who thought we wanted to trade."

"They have no weapons." Einar scratched his graying

beard and frowned. "And so many of them. Look at the way they mill about."

It wasn't uncommon for groups of men to meet Aksel's crew on the shore, unaware of the danger, but still with weapons to hand. This was far more than they'd ever seen, and there were women and children among them.

Aksel shrugged. "Just a mob of unarmed fools. So we chase them a bit."

*

"Where are these from?" Grace bent over the remains. Four bodies, three adults and one child.

"An island in the Channel called Portland," Dr. Livingstone replied. "We've uncovered evidence of Viking raids there before. This one dates to the early eighth century."

"Well, these wounds are consistent with weapon trauma from that period." Grace paused. "But there's so much of it."

"That confused me as well. I'm used to seeing fractures like this." Dr. Livingstone pointed to the skull of an adult female nearly bisected by a heavy bladed weapon. "But all these other wounds. To the limbs, to the ribs, I don't know what to make of them."

*

They were surrounded. Cornered. The people—though Aksel had stopped thinking of them as such—crowded in, hands reaching, slack mouths emitting an unearthly chorus of hungry moans. He drove his sword into the belly of a young woman, but she did not slow, and she clawed at his shield with terrible strength. He let go of the sword, pulled the axe form his belt, and chopped at her shoulders and neck. There was no spray of blood, no pained cries, just his blade biting into inert flesh.

Halfthor screamed somewhere behind him, long and terrible. The sound of a man enduring agony unlike any he'd encountered in this world or would in the next.

Aksel backpedaled, trying to shove the woman away with his shield. His feet tangled beneath him, and he went down on his back. Einar suddenly loomed behind Aksel's attacker, and his two-handed axe came down like a silver meteor. The huge blade split the woman's skull and she fell away.

The old warrior's face was grim as he pulled Aksel to his feet. "Hit them in the head."

*

"These aren't defensive wounds." Grace examined a humerus with three deep gashes. "They look postmortem."

"I agree, but why? Dr. Livingstone said. "Viking raiders killed, yes, but they were after gold and slaves. Savaging the bodies after death makes no sense."

Grace set the humerus back on the table. "Okay, these are the victims. Any chance you recovered remains from their attackers?"

A strange look passed over Dr. Livingstone's face. "This way."

*

Aksel was alone. His men lay dead and half-devoured on the beach. The townsfolk pressed in, mouths agape, clawing and biting. He swung his axe at the head of his nearest attacker. The blade bit into the skull and stuck there. The man fell backward, ripping the weapon from Aksel's hand.

He'd lost his shield, his sword, and now his axe. Aksel drew his knife and thought about slitting his own throat. They didn't give him the chance. The wall of bodies closed in, and he went down stabbing and screaming.

*

"Was the body in this state when you found it?" Grace asked. The headless skeleton of a large man had been reassembled on another table. An ancient chainmail shirt in surprisingly good condition lay next to it.

"You mean the disarticulation?" Dr. Livingstone said. "Yes. As you know, it's not uncommon for bodies to come apart in the ground, but this man was . . ."

"Ripped to pieces," she finished. "Are these . . . teeth marks?" She ran a hand along a tibia pocked with small gouges.

"They are, and they match two of the victims' skulls."

"Wait? You're saying these peasants killed this Viking and then *ate* him?" She no longer thought of the savaged remains on the other table as victims.

"I . . . don't know," Dr. Livingstone said. "But I have one more thing to show you."

He went to another table on which sat a metal box secured with a padlock. He removed the lock and raised the lid. Inside was a human skull with a thin layer of mummified flesh. It bore no visible wounds and its mouth gaped open, wide.

"Watch." Dr. Livingstone took a pencil from his shirt pocket and pushed it toward the skull. Its jaws snapped down, cracking the pencil in half, and continued to move up and down. It was chewing.

"What in the hell?" Grace took a step forward, still eager for a closer look.

"Don't get too close." Dr. Livingstone held up a hand, and his sleeve rode down, revealing a bloody bandage around his wrist. "It bites."

Bite Back

Jonathan stood at the edge of the swamp, the water still and dark, moonlight and fireflies playing across the glassy surface. He breathed the night air, fighting tears through the memories of the man he'd loved. He held out the urn, unscrewed the top, and let the wind catch the ashes and pull them over the bayou. The moment Nolan's remains touched the water, the deep rumbling call of a gator sounded in the dark.

"Here you are," someone said from behind Jonathan. The voice was rough, even grating, but somehow still alluring. "I didn't think you'd show."

Jonathan turned to face the wolfman. "I did it for Nolan."

In his human form, the monster who called himself Kissinger stood a few inches taller than Jonathan's six feet. His long hair and ragged beard gave him a slightly unkempt look, but his dark eyes and sensuous lips lent him a feral beauty. "Which one was he? The big, husky guy who sounded like a redneck?"

Jonathan looked away. Nolan *had* been a big, husky guy, but also smart, gentle, and so different from the ignorant assholes in this backwater town. They'd planned to leave Mississippi, go to California, and be happy, be together. Then they'd met a werewolf at a club in Biloxi. They hadn't known what Kissinger was, of course, until it was too late.

"You know who he was," Jonathan said. "That's why

you came. Because I got away."

A ripple of anger frayed Kissinger's smile at the edges, and his eyes flashed red in the gloom. "Your man was strong. I'll give him that."

"He was the strongest person I've ever known." Jonathan trembled at a sudden surge of pride. Nolan had been six-foot-eight and almost three hundred pounds, and he'd used all his size and power to hold a monster at bay so Jonathan could escape.

"Well, he's dead now." Kissinger's smile returned full strength, all teeth. "I ate pieces of him while you ran. Took my time."

"And I'll kill you for that," Jonathan said. The gator's call boomed through the swamp again. Closer.

"Kill me?" Kissinger laughed. "If your big, strong man couldn't do it, how will you? Do you even know how to kill someone like me?"

"Silver," Jonathan said.

Kissinger made an exaggerated show of looking around, shielded his eyes with his hand. "Well, my friend, I don't see or smell any silver."

"You're right. I don't have any, and I wanted to meet you at night, alone, because I knew *you* would come. I guess you don't leave witnesses very often. This isn't New York or Los Angeles. People believe in monsters here."

"Maybe you're right. So, what do you have planned? Got some buddies hidden? No, I'd smell them. You *are* alone."

"I have this." Jonathan pulled a Mason jar from his coat, one of six. He'd already dumped the other five along with six whole chicken carcasses into the water.

Kissinger didn't flinch at the movement. He was truly unafraid. "Whatcha got there? A Molotov cocktail?"

It occurred to Jonathan he might have used fire, but he had something better in mind. Something his Daddy had warned him about since he was old enough to stand and wander to the bayou's edge. "Nothing like that." Jonathan unscrewed the cap from the Mason jar.

Kissinger sniffed. "Chicken blood. Sorry, not my brand."

"It's not for you," Jonathan said. "Not entirely."

"You are *really* starting to bore me." Kissinger stepped closer, reaching. "If you don't struggle, I'll make it—"

Jonathan flung the contents of the Mason jar, splashing his foe with a quart of chicken blood.

Kissinger stopped in his tracks, eyes bulging. Jonathan retreated slowly to the water's edge.

The gator rumbled.

Blood dripping from his beard, Kissinger's face twisted, changed, the bones and sinews cracking as a muzzle pushed and distorted his human features. Gray fur burst through his clothing, which ripped and fell away. His jaws gaped wide, bone-white fangs gleaming in the moonlight, and he unleashed a long, shuddering howl. The transformation from man to monster took only seconds, and then Kissinger charged, low to the ground.

Jonathan refused to look away or close his eyes. He'd face his death like Nolan. Strong and brave.

The water erupted in a dark spray when Kissinger was nearly on top of Jonathan. A low-slung, scaly body burst from the swamp. The gator, a massive bull, slammed into the charging werewolf and clamped its huge jaws around one leg.

Kissinger loosed an angry roar and tried to wrench free, but even the lycanthrope's strength was no match for a thousand pounds of hungry reptile. The gator dragged its prey back toward the water, tail thrashing in the mud. It reached the water, and a chorus of rumbling and hissing filled the swamp. A dozen other floating, scaled shapes loomed beyond the shore.

Jonathan sank onto the cool, mossy sward and watched the water churn white. The werewolf roared again as the other gators joined the feast, pulling, rolling, ripping.

After a time, the swamp quieted, and the fireflies resumed their bright dance. The gator loosed one last, distant rumble, soft and forlorn.

Jonathan smiled through fresh tears, kissed his fingers, and dipped them into the still water.

Little Sister

Daddy made Little Sister for my seventh birthday. He made her from part of me that got hurt in the accident. He took little pieces of what I lost—he said it was tiny, tiny things called DNA—and put them into her. He said when Little Sister came out of his lab, she'd be like me, only with legs. She could push my wheelchair, read to me, and help me take a bath.

Little Sister didn't come out like Daddy said. She didn't look like me. She didn't even look like a person.

Daddy said Little Sister wasn't what he promised. He was sad because he wanted her to help me. He said he would put her to sleep and try again. I knew that going to sleep meant she would die, like our dog Buster did when he got old. I told Daddy I wanted to see Little Sister. He said no, but I cried and fell out of my wheelchair. It hurt and he was sorry, so he showed me.

When Daddy pushed my wheelchair into the lab, I could feel Little Sister in my head, like a thought that wasn't mine. She was in a clear plastic cage on one of Daddy's tables with a lid and a lock on top. Lots of people would think Little Sister is gross or scary, but I loved her because she was broken, like me. She looked like a fat worm with skin the same color as mine. Her head had no eyes or ears, just a mouth with sharp teeth inside, but I knew she could hear and see me.

That first time I saw her, she lifted her head and made a sound. It was like when a kitty meows, but softer and almost like it was my voice. That surprised Daddy, and then he said lots of things about his work I didn't understand. He said Little Sister was like a *larva*—that's a baby bug—that will never grow up and be what it is supposed to be. He said he wanted to put her to sleep so she wouldn't hurt anymore.

I yelled at Daddy that it was bad to kill Little Sister because she was hurt and not perfect. I said that he should kill me, too, then, because I'm not perfect, and I hurt all the time. That made Daddy cry like he cried when Mommy died. I was sad, but I didn't want him to hurt Little Sister. I said I would take care of her, and he could show me how. He didn't want to, but he said yes.

Daddy lets me take care of Little Sister. It's sometimes hard. Her skin is very soft, and I have to put Vaseline on it so it doesn't dry out. Daddy said if her skin gets too dry it would hurt her. I have to feed her, too. She eats mice and hamsters, and I used to hate watching her eat because the mice and hamsters cried when she bit them, and she made a mess when she chewed them up.

I can always hear Little Sister thinking in my head, and that means I'm never alone, even when Daddy is working. Her thoughts are only colors or sometimes pictures, but I can feel when she's hungry or even hear and see what she does. I don't tell Daddy I can hear Little Sister thinking. I'm scared if he knew, he would take her away. He sometimes says she is too much responsibility and that she would be better off with the people at his work. They could learn things from her, he says. I tell him no, and he listens for now.

I think Little Sister scares Daddy. She scares me sometimes, too. She figured out how to open her cage and get out. She does bad things at night when I'm sleeping. Last week, she ate my kitty, and I felt her do it in my dreams. I heard and saw my kitty crying when Little Sister bit him. I even tasted him when she swallowed him whole.

I tell Little Sister she can't do bad things, but she doesn't understand. I worry she might get out of our house. I lock my bedroom door at night, and Little Sister can't open it. She's not big enough. Daddy says she won't get bigger, but I'm not sure anymore. There are little nubs on Little Sister's body now that weren't there before. They look like little feet or hands. Daddy hasn't seen them, but I think they're growing. I think Little Sister is growing, too.

Little Sister had an awful thought today. A thought that scared me so much I don't know what to do. Through my bedroom window, she saw Mrs. Keller with her new baby, and I saw in my head Little Sister wanted to eat the baby.

I got so scared I almost told Daddy. I didn't because after Little Sister ate my kitty, I have been eating bad things too. I started with one of Little Sister's mice. It was furry and its little claws hurt my mouth, but I liked the way it squished and crunched, just the way Little Sister likes it. I asked Daddy for a new kitty, and he bought me one. I named her Tinkerbell, and Little Sister and I shared her. She tasted so good.

I can't tell Daddy what Little Sister's thought about the baby, not just because I ate a mouse and a kitty. Not just because he might take her away. I can't tell him because I had the same thought, and I was so hungry.

What Binds Us

I notice the pea-sized bump on the back of my hand when I put the key in the lock and open the door. I ignore it mostly because Steve is still sitting on the couch in a blanket shroud and watching *The Office* for the six-hundredth time. The place is a mess, sink clogged with dishes, trash overflowing, takeout cartons carpeting the floor. The litter box is the worst, though. The piss ammonia smell waters my eyes and pushes rage, hot and acrid, surging into my brain. It's *his* fucking cat, and dumping the litter is the one thing I asked him to do.

"Why didn't you clean out the litter box?" I say, trying and failing to keep my voice steady, calm, non-confrontational. The raised cyst or whatever it is on the back of my hand quivers.

"I don't feel good," Steve says, not looking away from the screen.

I kick empty Coke cans and food-stained Styrofoam out of the way and stand in front of the TV. "I said, why didn't you clean out the litter box?" I have to raise my voice to be heard over Michael Scott and company.

The slight increase in volume is all the ammunition Steve needs. He throws back his blanket with an exaggerated flourish, like a man doffing a cape before he begins a duel. He's been spoiling for a fight, just like me. "Don't fucking yell at me, Kelly." He starts with an old favorite: play the victim. Poor abused, put-upon Steve. "I told you I don't feel good."

I open my mouth to let the pent-up fury pour out, and then I see the growth on his cheek, bigger than the one on my hand. A silky tendril, white, a little thicker than a hair, juts from the raised flesh. "Your cheek," I whisper.

He saw my mouth move but didn't heard the words. "You're an hour late. What kept you? Drinking again or fucking another of your coworkers?" His words are carefully chosen and laced with enough truth to strike hard.

"That was two years ago," I say, a shame-filled mantra I've been repeating almost daily. The cyst on my hand quivers again, and a trickle of warmth runs along the back of my palm. I glance down. The skin has split open and weeps clear fluid. A tiny white strand squirms free of the growth, moving toward Steve like a seedling feeling for the sun.

"And two years later you still won't take responsibility for it." Steve stands, and the light from the TV reveals the growth on his face is not alone. There are three more, clustered on his forehead, each the size of a nickel and erupting with waving filaments.

I stumble backward in disgust, trip over an Amazon box, and go down on my ass. The pain sparks anger in me so huge I'm sure my skull will split open with it.

"Motherfucker!" I howl and half a dozen growths, maybe more, sprout on my chest beneath my shirt. They burst open like new sores, warm and wet and awful. This should terrify me, but instead it's like someone has injected pure fury into my blood.

Steve stalks toward me. "What the fuck did you call me?" Each rage-fueled syllable sends filaments shooting out of his face like silly string. They jerk and dance in the air between us.

Fabric tears as my own growths disgorge spidery filaments and push through my shirt with the zippering sound of tearing fabric. I climb to my feet, body trembling with adrenaline. "I didn't *call you* a motherfucker," I seethe. "Because what you are is worthless sack of unemployed shit who is destroying his life along with mine!"

The strands wriggling from the growths pockmarking our bodies make contact and intertwine. They coil around each other and pull us close, almost into an embrace. Steve and I stand nose to nose, close enough to smell each other's breath. The revolting stink of Doritos and coffee on his, the damning alcohol vapors of two Jack and Cokes on mine.

"Destroying your life?" Steve's eyes go wide in shock and disbelief. "You're the one who cheated. You did this to us."

The strands holding us tighten further. My vision swims and breathing becomes difficult. I still find enough wind to shout. "Well, forgive me for seeking comfort in the arms of someone who isn't a total fucking loser!"

Our bodies writhe and squirm. Pain lances through me as the tendrils grip and crush. It only makes me angrier. I throw back my head and loose a wordless shriek. The world dissolves into a choking red cloud of hatred, like a noose tightening around my throat.

*

I wake suspended in the middle of the room, caught in a web of white strands that fill the apartment like spider webs. Steve's body presses against mine, and we are wrapped tight in stringy filaments.

Steve moves, and at first, I think he is trying to free himself; instead, he brings his face close to mine. "Kelly," he whispers. "I . . . I'm sorry."

The tendrils' grip slackens, and they withdraw slightly into the pimpled growths covering our bodies.

I stare at my partner of the last five years. His face is barely visible in the lattice of organic wisps and coils, but there is sincere remorse in his eyes, and it should evoke the same in me. It doesn't.

"Fuck . . . you," I hiss, scarcely able to move my mouth enough to form the words. The tendrils squeeze, seemingly in delight. The breath leaves my lungs in a single agonizing blast, my ribs snap like rotten twigs, and I go into the dark on a black comet of wrath.

The Night, Forever, and Us

I slip through the window of my wife's room, the mingled smell of sickness and disinfectant sharp in my nose. The only sound is the low susurrus of hospital machines monitoring the failing systems of Lucy's body, charting their inevitable collapse.

They put her in hospice care two weeks ago. I am almost too late.

I approach her bed, despair and the bright urgency of my discovery warring within me. It's been six months since the diagnosis and two since I left. I still remember Dr. Wagner's face, his eyes, how hopeless they were. He delivered the news gently, but we knew a death sentence when we heard one.

We tried everything, borrowed and spent money for experimental treatments with a one-in-a-thousand chance of working. None of them did, of course, and Lucy accepted the inevitable, made peace with it. I couldn't. I searched for other remedies, grew desperate, and it led me away from her. It led me into the dark, and, finally, to the ruins of an ancient monastery on the border between Armenia and Azerbaijan. Within the crumbling edifice of black stone, I encountered a stooped monk, a pale creature who had not glimpsed the light for decades, maybe longer.

There, in the dark and quiet, I made a bargain that seemed inconsequential for what was offered. Maybe that decision will damn me, but I seized up on it and carried it with me back across the ocean.

I sit on the edge of my wife's deathbed and whisper, "Lucy. I'm here."

She turns her head, and her eyes flutter open. Her face is sunken, and her jagged cheekbones jut out against paper-thin skin. She wears the pink bandana I gave her months ago to cover the ravages of chemo. Only her eyes belong to her, cloudy blue but still clinging to life.

"Danielle?" she gasps. Tears slide down her face, each one an accusation I can barely stand. I left her alone when she needed me most. Neither of us had any family. Hers passed away when she was a child. I was a product of the foster care system. We had one another and nothing else. Two desperate souls who came together in the chaos of a world that should have twisted us both into human wreckage. No matter what happens tonight, my decision to leave will haunt me forever.

If Lucy could've summoned the strength, she might've struck me or raged at my selfishness. I would've accepted it, welcomed it for my sins. But she is long past such things, and she reaches up to touch my face. My own tears come, and I am thankful she cannot see their color in the dark.

"I'm so sorry I had to go. Nothing could help you here, but . . ." I nod at the night beyond her window. "I found something to make you well again."

A sad, tired smile overtakes her face. "Danielle, you ran. . . because you couldn't accept it, and I hated you." She grimaces with the effort it takes to choke back a sob. Her eyes cloud. "But I don't care anymore. I just want you with me."

I take her hand and kiss it. "What if there is no end? What if there doesn't have to be one?"

She sighs and turns away. I can tell even these small movements tax her. "No more treatments. I want to rest."

"Lucy, look at me. Really look at me."

I gently turn her head and lean forward into the moonlight streaming through the window. Despite her bottomless fatigue, Lucy's eyes widen. "What did you do?"

"Don't be afraid. I did it for us, for you."

"Your eyes," she says.

My eyes were blue before my trip to the Caucuses, like a winter sky. They are the color of the fading sun now.

"I know it's strange, but I don't feel pain. I don't fear sickness. All that's missing is you."

"What . . . what are you saying?

"Be with me." I touch her cheek. She flinches, maybe noticing for the first time how cool my skin is.

She reaches up and grasps my hand with surprising strength. "I'm scared, Dani."

I want so much to soothe her. "I love you, Lucy, more than life, more than death. Trust me. Please."

She shudders. Her face contorts and her mouth trembles. "It hurts. Can you make it stop?"

"I can."

*

Thirty minutes later, Lucy rises from her deathbed. She stands in the moonlight, a pale specter so lovely my soul aches to look at her. Her hair has returned, falling around her shoulders in a cascade of liquid black. Her body has regained its flesh, her face its proper contours, and her eyes burn a soft red, like mine. She doesn't appear sick anymore, she glows with dark purity, stark and beautiful.

I hold out my hand. Our cold fingers intertwine, and I kiss the top of her head, like I used to do and will do for a thousand years to come.

"What's out there?" she asks, excitement and wonder in her voice.

I push open the window and smile in the dark. "The night, forever, and us."

The Father of Terror

It starts with the dogs.

They show up a few days before a new hole appears, sleek, black things with long, narrow snouts and yellow eyes, skulking through the dark and howling at the moon. I think they sing to him, maybe to give him the strength to make a new hole. If I let them, they might even make him strong enough to come out of that hole. Then we'd be fucked.

Each year around the same time, as summer gives way to autumn, I have a dream about where the next pit will be. I don't know who sends these visions or whatever; maybe another god, a nicer one that doesn't want to destroy the world and all us humans in it. The first dream named the thing that could end all things. It's called Abu al-Hol. I found out later that name meant "Father of Terror." The Egyptians even built a monument to it, maybe to keep it from eating them. It's still there, thousands of years later. People call it the Sphinx now.

The dream came again three nights ago, and it showed me a place green and wet and cold. I used to get precise locations, like coordinates in my head, but the last couple of times it's only images. I got lucky; I recognized the place I was being shown, a park in a boring little town east of Seattle called Bellevue. So that's where I'm at, in the middle of the night, hunting dogs that look suspiciously like jackals.

Bellevue has one thing going for it—the town is wealthy and quiet. That means no cops, which is good.

The silenced .22 pistol I'm carrying under my rain poncho and the dead dog in a bag over my shoulder would be very difficult to explain.

Part of me hates shooting the dogs—I would never hurt an animal under any other circumstances. But these are different. These are *his*. I have to kill at least three for the ritual, to keep him quiet for another year. The dream told me how to do that, too: what words to say, to use a bronze knife instead of a steel one, that kind of thing. It's some kind of magic, and my Christian upbringing says I'm dealing with the devil, but better the devil you know than the one who might come out of a hole and eat the whole fucking world.

There are a lot of parks in Bellevue, and in one of them Abu al-Hol will open his pit. I'm headed there now, working my way through dark streets in the rain, eyes on the lookout for more of his dogs. I shoot two more. The Ruger, loaded with subsonic ammo, makes no more than a soft clicking noise when I pull the trigger. That gives me three. It's enough.

The park is small and secluded, sheltered from the street by lots of trees. There's an empty baseball diamond, a sandbox, and a basketball court. I know the pit is in the outfield grass. I can smell it—rotten meat and sulfur.

The new hole is about six feet across, and wisps of mist or steam rise up from it. It's so black it looks like it's painted on the grass. It's bigger this time.

There are three of his dogs around the pit, lithe silhouettes loosing high, wavering cries into the night. I pull the Ruger and snap off two shots. One hits. Two dogs race off into the night, and a dead one drops into the hole. That pisses him off. The ground shakes, and I can feel Abu al-Hol's anger in my head like a swarm of bees. No matter how many times I do this, shut him down, keep him from coming out of the ground, it scares the shit out of me. He isn't called the "Father of Terror" for nothing.

I don't look into the hole as I set my sack on the ground. The pit he opens connects to wherever he's trapped under the ground, and you can see straight down into it. The one time I looked, I saw his eye—yellow like a rotten moon and the size of a manhole cover—staring up at me. I didn't sleep for a month.

I say the words to the ritual. They don't sound like any language I've ever heard. I've tried sounding them out and writing them down, but even the internet couldn't tell me what they mean.

When I'm done with the words, the ground shakes again, harder. I pick up the bag, open it, and dump the dogs on the ground. This is the worst part. I gut each one with the bronze knife, then toss them into the pit. These are his sacred animals and throwing their defiled bodies back to him seals the deal. At least that's what I believe.

The hole begins to shrink, collapsing in on itself, and the presence of Abu al-Hol fades from my mind. He leaves something awful behind, something that guts my relief at stopping him again. Just before the hole closes, Abu al-Hol's rage subsides, and something far more terrible lurks behind it: a demon's hope wrapped like serpents around two words. *Next year.*

Stall Number Two

There's a gateway to hell in the men's room at Cory's Pub & Suds. It's in the second stall, and you have to shut the door and sit on the toilet for it to work. One minute you're squatting on the john, the next you're in the netherworld.

I went there by accident the first time. I guess everybody does. I was mixing beer and whiskey, and it always gives me the shits. So there I was in stall number two, painting the bowl like Jackson Pollock, when everything went dark.

When the lights came back on, I was standing in a bar—not Cory's—a cool, divey place like I remember when I was kid in San Francisco. A band played on the stage, and rocking music and happy people filled the joint. That music was something. The singer looked like Jerry Garcia, and the guitarist was the spitting image of Hendrix.

I stood there, holding my pants up like an asshole, when this guy came through the crowd. He wore a sharp black suit with a red shirt underneath, and his face was all angles and cheekbones. Good-looking doesn't begin to describe him. He stuck out his hand and said, "Hi there, Boyd. I'm the devil."

I shook his hand, warm and smooth. "The devil?"

"That's right. Satan, Old Scratch, Beelzebub," he said with a toothy grin. "Around here folks call me Lou."

I looked behind me, and I didn't see Cory's, just a sign

for the men's room. "Is this . . ."

"It sure is," Lou said. "But don't worry about that. You can leave whenever you want. Just go back through the men's room there, cop a squat in the second stall, and you'll be back where you started."

The band was doing "Touch of Grey," one of my favorite Dead songs. It was perfect, better than I'd ever heard.

"Or you can stay," Lou said with a sly grin. "Janis is on next."

"But I gotta give you my soul, right?" I took one halting step back toward the bathroom.

"Yeah, I have to charge a cover for the good stuff," Lou said. "But not as much as you think. Just a sliver of your soul. You won't even miss it."

"Really? How many slivers do I have?"

He eyed me like a guy might size up a used car he wants to buy. "You've got a nice healthy soul, Boyd. I'd say you can spend a hundred slivers or so before, well, before we need to make other arrangements."

I'd been spending the last ten years with my ass glued to a barstool at Cory's. Divorced, alone, in debt up to eyeballs, and mostly just watching the years slide away toward a death I'd started to wish would hurry the fuck up. Now I was listening to fucking Jerry Garcia and Jimi goddamn Hendrix live. I mean, it was only a sliver of my soul, and I could watch two of the greatest musicians ever.

"How much are the drinks?"

Lou smiled. "Complimentary."

That sealed it. "Okay, I'll stay."

91

"Excellent." Lou leaned forward and kissed me on the forehead. I felt a little woozy, and he put out a hand to steady me. "That's it. Enjoy the show."

That was three months ago. I've been back every night. Each time, it's a little different. Sometimes it's the dive bar and Buddy Holly is on stage. Sometimes it's a swanky joint and Sinatra is crooning. One time, it wasn't a bar at all. It was a baseball stadium, and I watched Joe DiMaggio hit a home run off Cy Young. The drinks were always free, and if I wanted companionship, and maybe a bit more, I got that too.

Trouble is, I haven't been feeling so good when I'm not at Lou's. I look in the mirror, and my face is all skinny, my eyes kind of dim and lifeless. I know why. Those little slivers of soul are adding up. A bunch of the regulars at Cory's have the look. It's funny; I never see those folks on the other side. Maybe Lou makes it special for each person, like their own private paradise.

I'm sitting at the bar at Cory's now, drinking a beer that tastes like ash, listening to stale, tinny music from the jukebox. Over at Lou's, the beer is cold and crisp, and the music is pure and wild.

Cory walks up to me, swishing his bar towel through the air. He looks good, alive, like he doesn't use the second stall in the men's room. He always knows what's going on down below. Maybe he has some kind of deal with Lou. "You headin' down tonight?"

"I don't know, man," I say. "Maybe I should slow down."

He shrugs. "Your call. 'Nother beer?"

I look at the flat, piss-colored liquid in my glass and

frown. "What's, what's he got running tonight?"

Cory smiles. "Boxing match. Joe Louis versus Rocky Marciano."

"No shit?" I'm a huge boxing fan. I guess Cory knows that.

"You know the drill. Show starts when you get there." He walks away, whistling, and stops to talk to another poor slob who looks like he's been spending a lot of time in stall number two.

I shake my head and push the beer away. I head to the men's room, telling myself I'm just gonna take a piss, but I know better.

Do Me a Favor

"I need you to shoot me in the head." Howard tapped his temple. "Right here."

Toby laughed and spilled beer down the front of his denim work shirt, then he saw Howard wasn't laughing with him. "What? Because some dude bit you?"

Howard glanced around the Suds Soaker. At twenty minutes to last call, they were alone except for Louise Hitchens, the Soaker's owner and sole bartender. She'd been tossing back shots of Maker's most of the night and wasn't exactly eavesdropping. "Not just some dude. A fucking zombie."

Toby laughed again, nervously, and took another swig of his beer. He'd polished off a dozen brews and lingered just south of totally shit-faced. Howard had pounded down fifteen, and he was frustratingly clear as a bell.

"How do you know it was a zombie?" Toby said.

Howard wasn't one-hundred percent certain it *had* been a zombie. He'd pulled over two nights ago to take a piss after he and Toby had closed down the Soaker. The old road had been dark like it can only get in the country, black and silent, as if you're the only person for miles. There he was, dick in hand, when something came out of the night, pale and awful and making a terrible moaning sound. He'd thrown one arm up to protect his face, and whatever it was bit him good. He'd pissed all over it and himself, and maybe that made it let go. Howard had raced home, and he hadn't left the house until tonight to ask an old friend for a special favor.

"Look, weird stuff has been happening," Howard said. "You notice I haven't used the facilities tonight?"

Toby frowned and then looked at the graveyard of empty beer mugs on Howard's side of the bar. "Hey, yeah."

"I haven't pissed or shit or done anything else a normal person should do in two days."

"Maybe you're just sick," Toby offered.

"No. Look." Howard rolled up his sleeve and held out his forearm. The bite still looked fresh, the teeth marks deep and pronounced. "No blood. No scabs. Nothin'."

Toby pushed his face close to Howard's arm, examining it with a drunken intensity. "Kind of looks like an animal bite." He brightened. "Maybe it was just a possum or something."

"Who ever heard of a person getting attacked by a possum?"

Toby shrugged. "Okay, a coyote then."

"It wasn't a fucking animal," Howard said. "I'm telling you it was a monster."

Toby blinked. "But I don't wanna shoot you. Who am I gonna go drinking with?"

"Look, man, I need you to do this because I can't do it myself. That'd be suicide, and you go to hell for that."

"Yeah, but I'd be a murderer, Howie." Toby swayed on his stool.

"Nah, killing a monster don't make you a murderer. Those guys on the *Walking Dead* ain't murderers, right?"

"Rick's a goddamn hero," Toby said fiercely.

Howard smiled. "Fuckin' aye he is. Just like you're

gonna be."

"Hey, assholes," Louise said from the other end of the bar. "It's three o'clock. We're closing."

"Keep your panties on." Howard hopped off his stool and tossed two crumpled twenties on the bar. "Come on, Toby, we're leaving.

*

Outside, Toby leaned against his F-150, still covered with rock dust from his workday at the quarry. His resolve had wavered since leaving the bar.

"I don't wanna . . ." He stopped, and his stomach loudly gurgled. Howard thought Toby might puke, but his friend fought the good fight and swallowed a mouthful of bile and beer.

"You still got that Ruger in your glove box?" Howard asked.

Toby looked away. "Maybe."

"Get it."

Toby unlocked his truck, leaned over the seat, and pawed open the glove box. He dug around until he found the revolver and showed it to Howard.

"It loaded?"

Toby fumbled with the cylinder release a few times but finally managed to open it. Five rounds of .357 magnum sat snugly in the Ruger's chambers. More than enough to do the trick.

Louise had made a beeline for her car after pushing them out the door. They were alone and the Soaker was out in the middle of nowhere. The shot wouldn't be heard by anyone that mattered. "Okay, you're gonna shoot me where I showed you, then take my body and bury it behind your barn."

"Oh, Jesus, Howie." Tears welled in Toby's eyes.

"I know, buddy." Howard put his hands on Toby's shoulders. "But I don't want to become a monster. I might hurt you or other good folks. You don't want that, right?"

Toby shook his head. "I guess not."

"So let's do it already. I don't wanna lose my nerve."

Toby drew in a deep breath and put the revolver against Howard's temple. He thumbed back the hammer. "I love you, Howie."

"Love you—"

The gun went off like a thunderclap, and Howard fell. *I'm dying*, he thought as he hit the ground. He lay there for a while, listening to Toby puke his guts out a few feet away and wondered why he was able to wonder at all.

He ran a hand over his temple. There should be a half-inch hole there and one about twice as big on the other side. He felt a burn mark, but beneath it the flesh perfect and unblemished. It didn't even hurt.

"Goddamn it," Howard said and stood up.

Toby whirled toward him, eyes as big as dinner plates. "You...you're not dead."

"Looks like you were right, Toby. I'm not a zombie." Howard paused, thinking. "You got any crosses at your place?"

Where They Belong

Daddy always says to put things where they belong. Toys have to go back in the chest. Milk has to go back in the fridge. Dead people have to go in the ground.

The gun is heavy, and I have to carry it with both hands. I had to figure out how to work it, how to make the round part pop out so I could put in the bullets. Before all the bad things happened, Daddy said I was too little to shoot. He said it would knock me down. I hope I am big enough now.

I carry the gun into the family room where Mommy is lying in front of the TV. I don't want to look at her because I might cry again. I can't cry now. I need to be a big boy so I can help Daddy. There is blood all over the carpet, and there are pieces of Mommy missing, the pieces Daddy ate. I walk past her into the kitchen without looking.

Anna is on the floor in the kitchen. She was so little that she couldn't even run when Daddy grabbed her. It doesn't bother me to look at her, though. I'm sad, but I didn't love Anna the same way I loved Mommy.

The basement door is next to the fridge, and it is open a little. I can hear Daddy in the basement. It sounds like he is moving things, heavy things, throwing them. I push open the door and look down the stairs. I don't like the dark, and I switch on the light. I have to stand on my tippy toes to do it. I'm scared Daddy might come up the stairs when the light goes on, but he doesn't. He is still moving around down there, making loud noises. It sounds like he is crying or breathing hard.

I walk down the stairs. I try to be very quiet because I don't want Daddy to hear me yet. At the bottom, Daddy is trying to grab Sylvester, our cat, but he is way back under the water heater and Daddy can't reach him.

"Daddy," I say.

Daddy turns around. He looks sick. His skin is gray, and his eyes are yellow. There is blood on his face and on his shirt. I know that blood is not his, and it makes my stomach hurt. He opens his mouth and yells or growls, like a monster. He doesn't say any words. I don't think he *can* say words anymore. I move up the stairs backwards.

"Come on, Daddy. Come out of the basement. Come be with Mommy."

Daddy follows me up the stairs and into the kitchen. I back up against the counter and hold out the gun with both hands. I aim it at Daddy. He walks toward me. His mouth is open and black stuff runs out of it. He reaches for me.

"I'm sorry, Daddy."

The gun jumps in my hand and makes the loudest sound I have ever heard. The bullet hits Daddy in the head and makes a big hole. Blood and yellow stuff, like oatmeal, splashes the wall behind him, and he stops walking. He stands there looking at me, but I don't think he sees me anymore. Then he falls down and stops moving.

I think it's okay to cry now.

*

It was easy to pick up Anna, but Mommy and Daddy were too heavy. I tried, but I couldn't get them outside. I got blood on my new shirt. It was one of my shirts for second grade. Mommy would be so mad if she knew, even though there's probably no school anymore.

I found the shovel in the garage. Digging was hard, and it took me a long time to make a hole in the backyard because I had to dig through the grass. I put Anna in the hole, and then I felt bad that she had to be in there by herself. I got Mommy's purse and Daddy's watch and the picture we took at Disneyland with all of us in it. I put them in the hole with Anna. Then I put the dirt in. I didn't want to put dirt on Anna's face, but I had to, and it made me feel a little better when I couldn't see her anymore.

When I finished, I went into the front yard. I can see the city, and there is a lot of smoke. Yesterday, or maybe it was the day before, I heard sirens, but now I don't hear anything but the wind. I wonder if other people will come to get me. I wonder if there are any other people left.

I go back into the backyard, and I lie down on top of the dirt where the hole was. I whisper, "Goodbye, Mommy. Goodbye, Daddy. Goodbye, Anna."

I remember what Daddy always said. Daddy, Mommy, and Anna are where they belong. I hope they go to heaven. I hope I go there too. I hope it is soon.

Night Walk

I watch the sun sink below the trees to the west, and I curse silently. I have no chance of reaching Delta Base before nightfall. Winter night comes quickly in the Northwest, and I'll be traveling in complete darkness for the last few miles. I stop walking on the crumbling asphalt of what used to be State Route 20 and set down my pack. I dig through its meager contents: a change of clothes, food, shells for the 12-gauge, and four candles and a lighter.

I rise and shove the candles and lighter into my pockets, then stuff everything back into the pack and throw it over my shoulder. I sling the shotgun. It had been quite useful against the bandits a few miles back, but it won't be worth a damn after sunset. The bandits' attack failed, but they may have killed me just the same: they delayed me so I can't avoid the night, and they broke my gas lantern. There had been three, two men and a woman, and I'd seen their clumsy ambush from a football-field away. I'd shot two of them as they broke cover but missed the last, and she'd knocked me down. I'd finished her off with my knife, but not before my Coleman had been reduced to glass shards and bent metal.

I think about stopping and building a fire—the dry forest floor offers no end of kindling—but one glance at the rainclouds gathering to the east and I dismiss the idea. I begin walking. The sun is now only a yellowish glow on the horizon, and the shadows cast by the trees spread long, dark talons across the road. The four candles might last long enough to get me to Delta Base, where they will have built bonfires to hold back the darkness, and the lurkers within it.

Only fire and sunlight keep the lurkers away. Light generated by any other source—be it a flashlight or a 1,000-candle-strength searchlight—won't stop them. When they first arrived, from God knows where, it took us too long to make that connection. Now the few remaining groups of starving humans work at survival during the day and huddle around roaring fires at night, just as our ancestors did tens of thousands of years ago.

Already, the shadows beneath the trees have taken on a disturbing liquid state that heralds the lurkers' approach. Minutes pass, and the road ahead grows dim and hazy in the onrushing dark. I debate for a moment whether or not to light a candle. A sudden shriek from the west makes the decision for me. I pull out one of the short, tallow candles. I flick the lighter with shaking hands and light the wick. It catches instantly, surrounding me in soft illumination.

I begin walking again, slower now. If I move too fast, I could blow out the candle. The forest on either side of the road is alive with howls and shrieks—the lurkers waking from their daylight slumber. They'll see my light, and although it will keep their shadowy claws from my flesh, it won't save me from seeing them. Looking at a lurker is like looking into the end of the world. Into death itself.

Ebon forms now flit between the trees, leaping in

frantic spurts of motion and leaving faint trails of black mist in their wakes. I keep walking, watching the road and watching the tiny lick of flame slowly devour the candle in my right hand.

The lurkers are all around me now, dozens of spectral shapes brushing against the invisible barrier of my light, whispering their hunger into my ears and filling me with dread. I push on, lighting my second candle with the first and tossing the still-burning nub behind me. I almost laugh as the lurkers in my wake scatter, shrieking as the light burns their wispy bodies.

I press onward, and I light the third and then the fourth candle as the miles pass. I'm still over a mile from Delta Base, and I know I'm not going to make it. I stop, and I can feel the lurkers absorb my despair. They stream around me, their tortured screeching filling the night. I feel sudden numbing cold against the back of my neck, followed by an ear-shattering howl. One of the lurkers has tried to reach through the barrier of illumination and grab me. My candlelight, feeble as it is, burned it.

I look up, and although the sky is dark with rainclouds, I haven't felt a single drop. My last candle is almost gone, and I have maybe five minutes of light. The towering trees beside the road sway with the passing of hundreds of lurkers, and their shrieks are an unending chorus of misery and death. I move quickly to the edge of the road and then off it. The ground is a mat of dried pine needles; they crunch beneath my feet. One chance. I close my eyes and drop the candle.

I wait for cold talons to tear through my flesh, but instead I feel warmth at my feet. I open my eyes and see a small blaze growing in the dried forest detritus. It spreads quickly—tendrils of flame lancing through the forest floor, sending lurkers screeching away from the rivulets of light.

One of the tall spruces nearby catches fire with huge whooshing noise, becoming a giant candle. Dozens of lurkers are instantly snuffed out by the explosion of fiery radiance. Now the heat hits me, and I stumble away from the conflagration I have created. I find the road again, and I run. As I pound down the cracked asphalt toward Delta Base, hounded by the shrieks of dying lurkers and the withering heat of the blazing forest behind me, I take some comfort.

Even if I don't make it, I'll die in the light.

Part III
Dawn

Masks

He has worked for Finco Novelties for as long as anyone can remember, a gaunt man with a slack, forgettable face and mud-brown eyes. Most of his coworkers cannot recall his name. Every day, he stands alone in the dusty room between the plant and the loading docks, his only company the soft, mechanical hum of the conveyor belt. For two decades, he has inspected the crude rubber masks produced by his employer, ensuring the demons, werewolves, witches, and ghouls fall within their admittedly low standards.

Finco is small enough he does not need an assistant, and the quality control he performs is only a token gesture. The dime stores and gas stations that buy Finco's products care only that they can be bought cheaply. Missing paint, flaws in the rubber, and other trifling errors do not concern them. His work is the hocus-pocus of a stage magician, a spell with no real magic.

Tonight, will be different. He has watched the sky for an alignment of stars and planets that heralds a gathering of power. Tonight, that power reaches a zenith, and his work will have meaning, his words will not be lost in the dust. He will be heard.

He has been at his post for five minutes, and the conveyor belt before him is silent and empty. He holds a tattered notebook in his right hand. It is filled with his other work, the fruits of his laborious studies—fumbling and amateur at first, but over the years sharpening into an instrument of exacting malice.

The conveyor belt shudders to life with a wracking mechanical cough. His shift begins.

The first masks to appear are painted a garish red, with wide fiendish features, small white horns, and a black goatee. Finco's Delightful Devil is one of their best sellers, and he is ready for them. He opens his notebook and reads an obscure passage from the *Dictionnaire Infernal*. His Latin is terrible, and the tortured, alien syllables of the words make it sound as if he is retching rather than reading. He feels energy gathering in the air, a smothering darkness that enfolds him, and when he says the demon's name aloud—*Adramelech*—he knows he has chosen the correct night for his work. He sees the demon's form outlined against the wall opposite the conveyor belt, a powerfully built man with a donkey's head and a vast plume of black feathers spreading behind it. He wonders if it will take his bargain or simply consume his soul. The demon obliges his command, and its vapory essence flows over and into one of the Delightful Devils crawling past on the conveyor belt.

He smiles. Adramelech was well-chosen. The child who dons its mask will be consumed by the demon of carnage and bloodshed. It will wear the boy's or girl's skin like an ill-fitting suit, using the flesh to feed its appetites until the body can no longer sustain it. He can only imagine what the demon might accomplish, what horrors it will unleash with its stolen body. He quivers with excitement, but there is still work to do.

He stands silently, watching the line of crimson faces slowly move past. It is an hour before the men in the plant switch over to the next mask, and they come trundling down the conveyor belt. Finco's Timid Tiger is a cartoonish representation of the great hunting cat, with huge eyes, a silly smile, and oversized teeth.

He flips a page in his notebook to another passage. This one is written in Sanskrit, the words pulled from a Vedic manuscript that took him a decade to find. Translating it cost him considerable money, time, and the pinky finger on his right hand. Learning to speak this ancient tongue had been more difficult than learning Latin, but he'd managed it, and as he grunted out the strange words, he knew it had been worth the effort.

The rakshasa was a different spirit than the infernal creature he had summoned for the Delightful Devil. Its malice was more subtle, its hungers more refined. He knows this shipment of Timid Tigers is bound for New Orleans, where they will be sold on Bourbon Street for Mardi Gras. The unsuspecting celebrant who dons this particular mask will find himself partaking in a party of a much different kind. The rakshasa will not likely kill its host, but the victim will be left with the memories of all the demon has done with its stolen body. Such memories are not the kind most men can live with.

The Timid Tigers soon finish, and the last of the night's masks begin rolling through. Johan the Yeti is bright white with tufts of faux fur framing an open mouth filled with big, square teeth. It is frightfully ugly and one of Finco's worst sellers.

He flips to the last page in his notebook and begins reading. The words flow with a rhythm that is beautiful yet ominous. As he finishes the Algonquin chant, the room grows cold and dark. The wendigo spirit hovers in the air above the masks, a terrible, emaciated specter of cannibalistic hunger. It flows into one of the Johan the Yeti masks as he commands, and he stops the conveyor belt.

He picks up the mask and slides it over his face. The wendigo surges into his soul, and he is filled with an all-consuming hunger. The demon leaves enough of his self intact that he will experience every bit of what is to come. This is what he wants, this is what he has worked for. He turns toward the factory interior, full of people who have shunned him for twenty years. Today they will learn his purpose. Today they will learn his power.

Today they will learn his name.

Cowtown

"Dude, again, chupacabras eat goats not cows," Miguel said and stepped over the barbed-wire fence, being careful not to snag his crotch. The field on the other side was dark, and hulking bovine shapes loomed in the moonlight.

His employer, Dale Costa, moved ten feet ahead, shining a flashlight into the gloom. He stopped, turned, and pointed the light at Miguel's feet. The powerful smell of garlic wafted through the air between them courtesy of the string of bulbs Dale wore around his neck.

"I don't think garlic works on them, either," Miguel said. They'd discussed this before, and though Miguel knew the legend of the chupacabra well—his abuela used to scare the shit out of him with it—Dale remained convinced the infamous goat-sucker of Mexican folklore was at the root of his problems.

"Look, man, something's eatin' my cows," Dale said. "Maybe it's not a by-the-book chupacabra, but it's gotta be in the same family or some shit."

Dale had fifty head of cattle on his dairy, and losing one cow was bad, but he'd lost four, and that was outright catastrophic. Miguel had joked, perhaps inappropriately, after they'd found the first cow, torn open and drained of blood, that maybe it was some breed of northern chupacabra. Had he known his employer's predilection for wild internet conspiracy theories, he would have kept his mouth shut.

Miguel shook his head. "So, we're gonna, what? Kill it with garlic and a shotgun?"

Dale carried his 12-gauge in his left hand, loaded with shells filled with silver BBs. Miguel had told him silver was for werewolves, but he hadn't listened to that either.

Dale blinked. "Well, yeah. I figure the garlic'll make him weak, then I'll blast him."

"Then what am I doing here?"

"I need a positive ID once I nail the little bastard. You've seen a chupacabra before, right?"

Miguel shook his head. He hadn't ever seen a chupacabra because they didn't exist, but Dale had promised to pay him five hundred bucks. Now that he was out here, though, the reality of the situation came crashing down.

"Dale," he said. "Look, it's not a chupacabra killing your cows. It's people, and the kind of people that can do that to an animal can do it to us. Get it?"

"Horseshit," Dale said. "Nobody in Modesto would do that. This is a good Christian town, not some pit of devil-worshipers like San Francisco or Sacramento."

"Listen, man," Miguel said. "I'm from Modesto too, and there are some bad motherfuckers in this town. We need to call the cops."

Dale's eyes narrowed. "You want that five hundred bucks or not?"

Miguel really needed the money. He was getting behind on his child support, and five hundred would put him square with his ex. He reached around and touched the butt of the Sig Sauer P226 stuck in his waistband. He'd loaded it with plain old copper-jacketed lead, and it lent him some comfort.

"Fine, you got half an hour."

Dale nodded. "Then turn on your flashlight and help me look."

Miguel switched on his Maglite, and they moved further into the field, passing sleeping cows oblivious to the humans in their midst. Cows did not, as urban myth attested, sleep standing up, and when Miguel spotted one on its side, the first real stirrings of fear uncoiled in his guts.

"Look," Dale whispered, and pointed his shotgun at the cow Miguel had spotted. As they moved closer, Miguel realized the animal was moving, jerking and twitching—something else was moving it.

Miguel pulled the Sig from his pants. Whoever it was must have seen their flashlights, and the fact they hadn't run off was a bad sign.

"Turn off the flashlights," Dale said, hitting the switch on his. He crouched low and took his shotgun in both hands.

Miguel turned off his Maglite and pointed his pistol at the prone cow. Dale saw the gun and nodded. "Good thinking," he said. "Your bullets will slow it down so I can get a good shot."

"Dude, please listen to me. That is not a fucking chupacabra," Miguel said. "It's some crazy Satan-worshiping assholes. Let's just go and call the cops."

Dale scowled and shook his head. "I told you, people in Modesto don't do that." That apparently settled the matter for Dale because he moved off toward the stricken cow and put his shotgun to his shoulder.

Miguel followed behind Dale, a little to his right, so he'd have a clear shot at the loony son-of-a-bitch gutting cattle in the middle of the night.

They were within ten paces of the cow when it stopped moving. They waited, and the hairs on Miguel's arms stood on end. He opened his mouth to tell Dale he was five seconds from leaving his ass in this field, when two dark shapes darted away from the cow, running east and west. The thunderous roar of Dale's shotgun followed, and startled Miguel so badly he fell over on his ass, firing his Sig into the air. He climbed to his feet and saw Dale sprinting after his targets. Miguel followed in a shambling run.

He caught up to his employer, who had stopped in the middle of the field, his shotgun resting casually over one shoulder. The dairy farmer stared down at something in the tall grass. "Got one," Dale said happily and switched on his flashlight.

Dale's light fell across something with leathery gray skin and a bulbous head. Two massive, black eyes stared up at them, and the creature's toothless mouth hung slack in death. Miguel's bladder let go in a hot, wet rush as he realized what he was seeing.

"Goddamn it," Dale said, shaking his head. "Sorry, Miguel. Not a chupacabra. Fuckin' aliens again."

Bear Necessity

At the sound of a knock on his door, Jerry nearly jerked the shotgun's trigger and blew his TV to atoms. He swallowed, clicked the safety on the Mossberg, and got up from the couch.

"Who is it?" A dark shape blotted out the stained-glass panes in his door.

"It is Uri," came the reply in a thick Russian accent.

"Are you, uh, the bear guy?"

A soft chuckle. "Yes, I am the bear man."

Jerry unlocked and opened the door. The man standing on his stoop looked to be part bear himself. He was tall, muscular, with a great black beard and a bald head. He smiled and his teeth shone like pearls through the dark tangle of hair on his face.

"Ah, Mister Harris. I am Uri Shostakovich. I have come to help you."

"Thank god," Jerry said. "Your cousin recommended you."

Uri's smile widened. "Ivan is good boy. Now tell me about your problem."

Jerry pointed to the barn on the other side of his expansive property. It was quiet, but too big for him to manage alone. He paid four men to cut the huge lawn and keep the grounds shipshape. "Um, a drifter got on the property yesterday. Harold asked him to leave, but he went nuts and attacked, like biting and stuff. Harold got sick first and I guess he spread it to Jonathan, and then Jonathan must have gotten David or Jesse . . ." He began to shake again.

Uri put a heavy hand on Jerry's shoulder. "Don't worry. Uri is here. Now, please put your weapon back in the house."

"Oh, are you sure?"

"I have something better than shotgun." Uri nodded toward his vehicle parked in the driveway, a diesel truck towing a livestock trailer.

"I will go get them, and we will begin." Uri went to the back of his trailer, opened it, and pulled down a ramp. A musky animal smell wafted out.

"Sasha, Baba Yaga. Come. There is work to do." The trailer rocked, and two black shapes appeared. The bears were enormous, ambling things. Both came out on their hind legs, walking upright. The first, Sasha, Jerry supposed, towered over Uri, who had to be a good six-five. The second bear, Baba Yaga, towered over the first. Its dense fur made it look like a giant ink blot against the blue summer sky.

"Ah, my darlings," Uri said. The bears walked up to him, dropped to all fours, and licked his face like terrifying overgrown puppies. "Are we ready to dance?"

It was so bizarre Jerry couldn't help himself, though Ivan told him Uri didn't like too many questions. "Why bears, Mr. Shostakovich?"

Uri frowned, and one of the bears made an irritated huffing noise. "Because they are good at the work, and they do not become infected after, like dog or wolf."

Jerry wasn't exactly an expert on the infected and in no position to argue.

116

"Now, you will go to the barn, open it, and move away," Uri said. "Sasha and Baba Yaga will take care of the rest."

Jerry hadn't gone near the barn since he lured the four men in there with a dead cat and locked them away with a chain and padlock. He walked up to the barn doors, digging into his pocket for the keys. Behind him, music began to play, classical of some kind, maybe a waltz. He glanced back and realized the music was coming from the cabin of Uri's truck. The bears were moving in his direction.

As he neared, the barn doors bowed outward and the chain and padlock holding them closed rattled. A hoarse, angry cry echoed from the other side, and Jerry's bowels turned to water. He fumbled with the keys but managed to get the right one into the lock. The padlock fell away, and he turned and ran. The barn doors flew open.

Uri's bears moved toward him. They stood on their hind legs again, twisting and swaying to the waltz blaring behind them.

"Hurry, Mister Harris," Uri called from beside his truck. The bears flashed past Jerry, and he heard a guttural cry. Jonathan or maybe David.

He reached Uri, who grabbed him and spun him around. "Now, you see my darlings. How they dance."

The bears and the four infected came together as the music reached a crescendo. The bears' long claws and terrible teeth ripped into the men, though Jerry realized that calling them *men* wasn't quite right anymore. What the bears did to them was mercy more than anything. Sasha and Baba Yaga ripped limbs free and broke open skulls as the music played. It was over in under a minute, and the bears, gore spattered yet clearly satisfied, danced back toward them.

Uri turned off the music, and the bears dropped to all-fours and licked the blood from their paws. "Now, we must talk payment, Mister Harris. My fee is—" He paused and stared at Jerry's arm. "What is that?"

Jerry blinked and looked at the bloody gauze taped to his right forearm. "Oh, I scuffled with one of them getting him into the barn. He scratched me."

Uri's eyes narrowed and he reached into the cabin of his truck. The waltz thundered out again, and the bears rose up on their hind legs. "That is a bite, Mister Harris."

"No, it's a scratch." Jerry backpedaled and his feet tangled under him. He went down on his ass as Sasha and Baba Yaga swayed toward him. The bears closed in, towering, looming, and Jerry screamed and joined their dance.

The Grove

When I was a boy, the trees grew faster in the old grove behind our house. Faster than they should, faster than what you could call natural. They had a strange look to them, too, those trees. The patterns in the bark took on familiar shapes if you stared at them long enough, almost like faces.

The trees grew fast and took things from the ground, bits of furniture, an old tricycle, the skeletons of small animals. Once I saw the skull of a coyote sticking straight out of a branch ten feet off the ground. Grinning white teeth, eye sockets empty but still staring down on you like it was watching.

Daddy told us not to go into those woods or listen to the wind whistling through the leaves, rustling the branches like shaking voices. I didn't pay any heed to his warnings—too young, too curious. I would stand at the edge of the grove where the trees are still small and imagine they were talking to each other. Maybe they were.

My brother Johnny disappeared when I was ten and he twelve, and Daddy said the trees had taken him. I remember Momma telling him to hush with that talk or he'd scare us children. We grieved, and things were quiet for a while.

Then, Nancy, my little sister, disappeared six months later. When Momma went into town to arrange the funeral, to buy the empty box we would mourn over, she left me at home with Daddy. He was in a bad way, crying and cursing. I tried to calm him down, and I thought I did, but it wasn't calm. It was quiet resolve. He got an axe from the tool shed and went into the grove. I followed, begging him to stop and come back.

Daddy went deeper in, raving at the trees, hitting the big ones with the axe, making them leak sap like black blood. I heard the wind rattling in the branches overhead, scraping and scratching. The trees were talking, and as I hurried after Daddy, they seemed to close in, the canopy of leaves eating the sky like a green shroud.

When I caught up to Daddy, he stood at the base of a big tree, feet planted, swinging the axe with all his strength. Bits of wood chipped and flew, and that old black sap splattered the nice white shirt Momma bought him for the funeral.

I tried to stop him, but he shoved me away. "Look at it, David," he said. "Look at the thing that ate your sister. Can't you see her face?"

I didn't understand none of that, but it scared me, and I begged him to quit and come back to the house. The rattling in the branches got louder, and it sounded angry. Those trees weren't talking now, they were screeching their hate down at us.

A branch broke off from one of the boughs, big and heavy, and it fell on Daddy, knocked him down and pinned him to the ground. I tried to push it off, but I wasn't strong enough. It lay on his stomach, and blood ran out of his mouth. He told me to run, to get Momma and enough kerosene to burn the grove.

I did run, all the way home, the trees scraping and

scratching overhead. Sometimes it seemed the branches dipped against the wind, like they were gonna block my path. I pushed on until I reached the boundary of the grove and the grass beyond.

When Momma got home, I was in tears, terrified and ranting. She grabbed hold of me and held me until I stopped shaking, until I could tell her what had happened. It was dark then, but she grabbed a flashlight and told me we'd find Daddy, right now. I told her about the kerosene, but she wouldn't get it. She said it was Daddy's sadness talking, making him do terrible things.

We ran into the forest and it had grown quiet, the wind nothing but a trickling gust. When we reached the place where the branch had fallen, Daddy was gone. Momma called out for him, running around the spot where I'd left him, her voice echoing off the trunks. I stayed put, remembering what Daddy had said about the tree that had eaten Nancy. I looked up and caught a flash of white.

Daddy was half inside the tree, twenty feet off the ground. His head and arms dangled, and the rest of his body had been swallowed by the bark, like it had grown up around him, absorbing him into the heartwood. He was still alive, looking down on me, eyes bulging from their sockets, blood dripping from his mouth. I knew that the tree was eating him, growing as it sucked the flesh and blood from his body, just like that coyote I'd seen.

Momma found me soon after, grabbed me, and ran. I don't know if she saw what I saw, but she never spoke about that day, not even on her deathbed last year.

We moved away a month later, and I haven't been back in twenty-five years. I think about the trees often.

Do they still take things from the ground to carry off and eat? If I went back to the edge of the grove and listened, would I hear the trees talking with the voices of those they'd taken? Would I hear my father's voice? My brother's? My sister's? Would I want to follow?

Beyond the Block

The block gleams with congealed blood as I kneel before it. The headsman has been busy today—I'm the last of twenty. He towers over me, and his eyes, a surprising bright blue, gleam from the depths of his black hood. They are twin glaciers where it seems warmth or mercy can find no purchase. He takes one hand from the haft of his axe, places a meaty palm between my shoulder blades, and pushes me over, forcing my neck into the notch. The block is cold on my skin, and it smells of the butcher's stall, coppery and rank.

"Don't squirm," the headsman says, leaning down to whisper into my ear. His breath smells of onions and pipe weed. "Stay still, and the axe will bite clean." It is a kindness, this warning. Today I saw the axe crack the spine of a man who jerked forward to avoid the headsman's stroke. His pained howls still ring in my ears. I will be still.

I stare at the small crowd gathered before the gibbet. It has dwindled now; most have had their fill of death. Lord Magister Vyard is still there, of course, a gaunt scarecrow in black, the three-pronged sigil of his office glaring from his breast, blood red like the fading afternoon sun. Lucinda stands next to him, trying to look away. Vyard's thin fingers are locked around the back of her neck, keeping her facing forward. He wants her to see this. Vyard's lips are moving. I cannot hear what he says, but his mouth twists and draws violently as he utters some silent, hateful curse.

The headsman draws in a deep breath above me, and I hear the honed steel of the axe-head scrape away from the gibbet. The axe whistles down, and there is sudden, terrible pressure on my neck, just below the base of my skull. There is no pain as my head comes cleanly away from my body, just the strange vertigo of the world turning end over end.

My head rolls a few feet and stops, then I hear the heavy tread of the headsman moving in my direction. I open my mouth to speak but can make no sound.

The headsman's thick fingers twine through my hair, and he hoists me up for the crowd's appreciation. I have a clear view of the executioner's square. I see the crowd, I see Lucinda on her knees before a puddle of vomit, and I see Vyard striding forward. He holds open a black silk bag, and when he reaches the scaffold, the headsman drops me into it.

I plunge into darkness, and here I wait for death. I wait for sight and hearing to fade. I wait to behold the gates of heaven or writhe in the fires of damnation. I experience neither. I come to the strange and awful realization that my head lives apart from my body. This realization is quickly followed by another. Vyard is the Lord Magister, the king's most powerful sorcerer, a man to whom death is a paltry obstacle. For loving Lucinda, Vyard's young wife, he had me executed and now something much worse. The man's rages are feared throughout the kingdom, and his curses are more than angry words.

Light returns as I am pulled from the silk bag. The light is from a torch carried in the left hand of a man who is not Vyard. He holds my head in his right. I see a bare stone wall before me, and upon it a row of tall iron spikes. The man lifts me above the wall, and I see the executioner's square below and the city sprawling beyond. The height of my vantage point and the view tells me where I am—the Lord Magister's tower.

There is sudden sharp pressure—again, no pain—as the stump of my neck is forced down onto a spike. The man, a guard perhaps, grunts with the effort of forcing the iron barb through the meat and gristle. His task complete, he leaves me, taking the light of his torch with him.

This is to be my fate, to spend years uncounted as a ghoulish ornament upon my killer's wall. Vyard has condemned me to a hell of slow and certain madness, another victim of the Lord Magister's cruelty.

Before I can slip further into despair, I am aware of a strange sensation. A feeling outside the prison of my skull, like an old memory I can't completely recall. Then it crystalizes, and joy surges through me—I can feel my hands, my legs, my body! At first it is little more than a ghostly tingling, like an itch I can't quite scratch. Then the sensation intensifies, and I feel my fingers moving against soft and yielding resistance. I can see the empty square below and the pile of corpses near the gibbet. I focus on my body, forcing my legs to move, my arms to push. The pile of headless corpses in the square topples over, and among them is my own.

I tell my body to stand. It obeys my phantom urging, and I can feel solid ground beneath its feet. I carefully pilot my orphaned flesh to the gibbet, mount the stairs, and move to the block where my mortal life ended. I tell my hands to pick up the headsman's axe, and its dead weight feels like something I have long been without. It feels like power, and it feels like vengeance.

I turn my body toward the Magister's tower. Vyard will come to gloat soon, and when he does, all of me will be waiting for him.

A Man of Many Hats

As I follow the blond man across the street, I'm wearing a baseball cap. There's a logo on the front: a stylized D. I don't know which team that represents; I'm not a sports fan. What I do know is that my eyesight is much better than usual, and my right arm feels like it's made of stronger stuff than flesh and bone, like iron or steel. I have Superman's arm.

The baseball cap arrived in the same package as the other hats, appearing on my doorstep this morning at eight o'clock, just like always. I heard the thump as it hit my doormat, but, as usual, no one was there when I opened the door. Inside the package were three hats: the baseball cap, a camouflage army cap, and a white cloth headband with a Japanese symbol on it. There was also a heavy round stone, a pistol, and a picture of the blond man with an address and a time printed (not handwritten) on the reverse. The baseball cap had a sticky note attached to it. Written on the note in black Sharpie was the number one.

I hadn't known what any of this was for, the hats or the other things. That would come later. I had put the baseball cap on my head, put the rest in my bag, then headed downtown. I went to the address on the back of the picture at the right time and waited for the blond man to arrive. He did. Just like I knew he would. The addresses and times are always right.

I've been following the blond man for ten minutes. He doesn't know I'm behind him. If he did, he wouldn't walk away from the more populated center of town, under the bridge where it's dark and no one can see us. He's got a briefcase, and he's dressed nice, like a businessman: crisp white shirt, black slacks, and sports coat. Maybe they want what's in the case. I never really know what it is they want, or even who they are. I don't need to; I like our arrangement. They send the hats and the other things, and when I'm done, they send money, a lot of money. The closet is nearly filled with stacks of bills. I should buy something soon.

The blond man has stopped and turned around, and he sees me. He also sees he is alone and in a place where no one can help him. His eyes grow wide. Sometimes the people know I'm there to hurt them; other times they seem completely surprised. The blond man knows, and he turns to run.

Now I know what the baseball cap is for. Now I know what the round stone is for. Images and words flood into my head. Words like "four-seam grip," "windup," "come set," and "kick and throw." On the top level of my mind, I don't understand these words, but the lizard brain, the part that controls my body, understands them perfectly. My fingers close around the stone in a precise grip, and I bring my hands together at my waist, rock back on my left foot, then step and throw the stone as hard as I can. My arm feels good and strong as I release it, and from over sixty feet away, the stone strikes the blond man in the back of the head with a hollow THWOK! He falls to the ground.

I start forward, digging in my bag for the next hat. I come up with the headband. I flip the baseball cap off my head and put the headband on. Now I feel quick, nimble, and I really want to hit something, or better yet, kick something.

I rush forward as the blond man is getting to his feet. He has a pistol in his hand, and there is blood on the collar of his white shirt. He aims the pistol at me. My right hand shoots out and catches the blond man's wrist. I marvel at my own speed and precision. I twist the blond man's wrist back at a precise angle, and he gasps in pain and drops the gun. Still holding him, I lash out in a short powerful kick at the blond man's knee. The joint snaps, bending the wrong way, and he wails. I let go of his wrist, and he falls to the ground.

It is time for the last hat. I take off the headband, pull the camouflage cap from the bag, and set it on my head. Now I want the gun. I need the gun. I take the pistol from the bag, and I know everything about it. I hear words like "Sig Sauer" and ".45 ACP" and "headshot."

The blond man holds up his hands and says something in a language I don't understand. They didn't give me a hat for that. I point the gun at his head and he wordlessly opens his mouth. The gun bucks in my hand and unleashes a tremendous sound. I shoot the blond man in his open mouth, and the gray sidewalk behind him is splashed with red.

I take off the camouflage hat and put it and the gun back in the bag. I put the bag on the blond man's body. Tomorrow, the body will be gone, there will be no mention of his death in the news, and the bag will be on my back porch filled with money.

It's time to go home. I'm out of hats.

His Favorite Tune

Colton Jackson walked along a dirt road while the man ordered to kill him pressed the barrel of a gun into his back. Dilapidated buildings rose around them, crumbling structures that spoke of instant prosperity followed by instant destitution. The town was called Mineola, and it died a hundred and twenty years ago.

"Hey, Derek, let up with that thing," Colton said, glancing over his shoulder. "I'm not running."

The pressure on Colton's spine eased. Unlike a lot of hitmen, Derek Hitchens wasn't overly cruel. "You wanna tell me why we drove all the way in the fuck out here?" Derek asked.

"This place is important to me."

"Why? Nobody's lived here since cowboys and shit."

Derek was right, but the town had other charms. "My ancestors have history in Mineola."

"They lived in this town?" Derek asked.

Colton shook his head. "They robbed it."

Derek made an amused snort. "I don't give two shits about your family history, but Mr. Falucci said you get to pick the spot. So pick."

"There." Colton pointed to a building in better shape than the rest. Its batwing doors marked it as the town's saloon.

"Works for me." Derek steered Colton toward the saloon.

Colton began cracking his knuckles and flexing his

130

fingers, an old habit, a thing he did before he played.

Derek chuckled. "Your arthritis acting up, Colton? I got something that'll fix that."

Colton ignored him as they pushed through the saloon doors with a rusting shriek of ancient, unoiled hinges. Inside, the smell of dust and rot pervaded, but most of the furniture—round tables and plain wooden chairs—remained intact. The bar stood to the left, a long strip of buckled wood, and behind it a mirror so grimed with dirt and age it reflected only a dim shadow of the world.

A Chickering upright piano, remarkably intact, stood in the corner. The keys were yellowed, like the tusks of some long-dead beast, but it would play, and an audience would be waiting.

"You wanna die *here*?" Derek said, looking around.

Colton turned to Derek, and the hitman's narrow face crinkled in anger at the movement. His pistol was suddenly in Colton's face.

"Wait!" Colton blurted and held up his hands. "I just want to ask you a question."

Derek studied him with dark, deep-set eyes, eyes that held neither mercy nor compassion. "You got five seconds."

"See that piano over there?" Colton nodded toward the old Chickering.

"Yeah, so?"

"You know what I did for Mr. Falucci before I got into trouble."

Understanding spread over Derek's face like sunlight across a mountaintop. "You gonna play fuckin' jazz piano on that old shitbox?"

"I'd like to try. One more tune before the end."

Derek looked at his watch. "You're lucky Mr. Falucci liked you. You *should be* night-night in a hole somewhere by now."

"He did like me." Colton sighed and remembered standing before Falucci's desk, something like sadness on the big mobster's face. "Jesus, Colton, why'd you have to go and steal from me," Falucci had said. "Now I gotta find a new piano player, and there ain't nobody as good as you."

The reason he dared steal money from a killer and thug like Falucci was simple: he made good money playing piano at Falucci's nightclub in St. Louis, but not good enough for a three thousand dollar a week cocaine habit.

"One tune," Derek said. "If the thing even fuckin' works."

"Thank you." Colton cracked his knuckles again and walked to the piano. The stool was new, though he doubted Derek noticed that. Colton sat and placed his fingers on the dust-covered keys. He could feel the energy in the air, an electric buzz he felt every time he came back.

"Whatcha gonna play?" Derek asked, leaning against the bar.

"'Oh! Susanna,'" Colton said. "It's a favorite of someone I know."

"That ain't jazz," Derek said but waved his gun in a *get on with it* motion. Colton struck the first notes. They plunked hollow and thready but not off-key. He let the jaunty song build, let the energy rise in the saloon. The hair stood on the back of his neck, and he heard distant voices and the sounds of glass clinking and playing cards shuffling.

Derek glanced around, his killer's eyes narrowing. "What the fuck is that?"

Colton kept playing and dim outlines of people appeared and moved between the tables and chairs, shadows wearing clothing a century out of fashion.

"Stop playing!" Derek shouted, pointing his pistol in little darting motions at the specters sliding around the room.

Colton did not stop, even when Derek pointed his pistol at him. He did not stop because the specters had gained substance and detail, the men and women they had been now clear. A bartender in a crisp white shirt with a handlebar mustache. An elegant woman in petticoats, her hair framing her face with delicate auburn curls. A trio of rough-looking men around a poker table, one hand on their cards, one on a knife or pistol at their belts. The saloon was suddenly filled with characters from a century past.

A gunshot rang out, and Colton winced, expecting a large, bleeding hole to appear somewhere on his body. Instead, he heard a heavy thud.

Colton turned and saw Derek lying face up by the bar, blood pooling under him. A stocky cowboy with coal-black hair and holding a smoking revolver stood over Falucci's man. The gunslinger's shadowy face might have been Colton's, just ten years younger.

Colton walked over to Derek and squatted next to

him. The hitman's breath came in wheezing, bloody gasps, but his eyes were clear and alert. "Derek, before you die you should know Jackson is my stage name. Real last name is James. Also, I'd like you to meet my great, great, great grandfather."

The ghostly gunman tipped his hat, and his voice came in a thready whisper. "Name's Jesse."

The Right Piece

Ms. Krestnaya's shop smelled like black licorice, and the walls were lined with tall, rickety shelves that held hundreds of glass jars and vials. Most contained dried leaves or berries; others held strange powders and less identifiable substances.

"Is anyone here?" I said and walked into the middle of the store. The only light shone down from a dingy glass ceiling fixture. It shed a sickly glow over the room and seemed to sharpen the pungent stinks there.

I heard a sound behind a short counter at the back of the shop, like shuffling footsteps. A door, faded red, opened to disgorge the giant form of Ms. Krestnaya. I'd never seen a woman that big, both tall and wide. That mountainous size came with a price, though. She walked with a cane, as if the weight of her massive frame was too much for her legs to bear.

"Oscar Rodriquez," Ms. Krestnaya said and smiled. She looked to be in her sixties, but people in the neighborhood said she was anywhere from eighty to a hundred and eighty. "What brings you to my store?" She spoke with a slight accent. Maybe Russian, but it somehow sounded older than that, ancient even.

I didn't move; my legs had gone rubbery, my feet leaden. The rumors about Ms. Krestnaya were strange or downright bloodcurdling, but my *abuela* said this woman could help me, and I trusted her more than anyone.

"You must come closer, *kotik*," Ms. Krestnaya said. "I

only bite those who bore me. You"—she pointed a bony finger—"look interesting."

I touched the bruises that still colored my cheeks yellow and black. My hand brushed the bandage over my left eye and I fought the sudden, maddening urge to scratch beneath it. "My *abuela* said you could help me." I walked up to the counter. The smell of black licorice intensified.

"Your grandmother is wise and skilled." She chuckled. "We have traded secrets in the past."

"She said you could help me get back at the people who hurt me . . . and my brother, Marcel." My voice faltered.

"Such is possible," Ms. Krestnaya said. "Tell me of these people who hurt you."

I clenched my fists hard enough that my knuckles popped, sounding like firecrackers in the small, quiet space. My ribs ached from where they'd beaten me with nightsticks. My good eye still burned from the mace they'd sprayed me with. Of course, all that paled in comparison to what they'd done to my brother. They said Marcel had had a gun or a knife. They'd changed the official statement twice. Not that it mattered. Marcel was in the ground and the people who'd killed him walked free.

"His name . . . his name is Lieutenant Raymond Scott," I said.

Ms. Krestnaya nodded. "Your grandmother explained there is a price for my help, yes?"

My *abuela* had been very serious about this part. She had warned me that Ms. Krestnaya's help might be worse in some ways than letting Marcel's killers go free. "I know. I'll pay it."

"Then come with me." Ms. Krestnaya opened the red door and passed through. I followed her into a tiny room with concrete walls. There were shelves here too and glass jars like those in the front of the shop. I covered my mouth when I realized what was in them—bits and pieces of people floating in yellowish liquid. One jar held a thick index finger with hair still on the knuckles. I saw an ear in another and what appeared to be an entire mouthful of teeth in one on a top shelf.

"What are these?" I whispered. I knew the answer, but part of me needed to hear it out loud.

"The price, of course," Ms. Krestnaya said. "Those who grant revenge need a fitting sacrifice. A man steals from you, you give a finger to make him pay. Someone speaks lies against you, a tongue or teeth will suffice." She sat down on an old red chair in the middle of the room and stared at me expectantly.

"It's a curse, right?"

Ms. Krestnaya shrugged. "A good word. As good as any. You pay the price, and someone suffers. But they suffer worse than you. Always."

They suffer worse than you played over and over in my head. A terrible yet soothing lullaby or maybe a spell. "I want that."

"You gave only one name," Ms. Krestnaya said and cocked her head. "There were more who hurt you and your brother."

I nodded. "But *he* ordered it. *He* told them to search Marcel's car." I shuddered, my stomach roiling. "And *he* fucking watched while it happened."

"I understand," Ms. Krestnaya said. "What will you pay for vengeance against this *watcher*?"

My hand went to the bandage over my left eye socket. My *abuela* had worked as a nurse before she retired, and she had helped me. Made it as painless as possible and made sure it didn't get infected afterwards. I reached into my coat and pulled out an oversized pill bottle. Inside, the eyeball gleamed wetly through the orange plastic. I handed it to Ms. Krestnaya.

"Ah, an eye for the watcher. Very fitting." Ms. Krestnaya held the bottle up to the light. The hazel brown pupil—a color my girlfriend had once called pretty—was visible even through the plastic.

"Will he die?" I said, shaking with rage and something far more invigorating—hope.

Ms. Krestnaya smiled, her elephantine teeth ghastly. "Worse. He will be *seen*."

At the Seams

It's getting harder to maintain focus. If I let it slip for an instant, I'll lose something. Maybe just a fingernail or a clump of hair and maybe a whole lot more. I want to look down at the empty end of my pant leg where my left foot used to be, but I won't. I'd like to hold on to my right foot a while longer.

In the end, it's pointless. How long can you keep thinking about just one thing? That kind of focus is not really possible. The mind wanders. Other thoughts intrude, and you just can't—

There is sudden, blinding pain in my right hand. I look down and my right index finger now ends shortly after the first knuckle. The rest of the finger lies on the floor, twitching and flexing like a fat, flesh-colored worm. There's no blood, just a clean separation after the knuckle, as if my finger never possessed that extra two inches of meat and bone.

I jerk my eyes away from the rogue fingertip and imagine myself floating naked in a white void, arms and legs outstretched. I am completely intact, and my body is surrounded by a faint blue haze, which seems to keep my body parts connected to one another and prevents me from flying apart. This thought has kept me alive for the last six hours, sitting on the edge of my bed and staring at the wall. I'd like to get up and turn off the light. I think it would be easier to focus in the dark. I can't risk it though, the expenditure of thought required would likely cost me—

Searing agony on the side of my head. My right ear lands in my lap with a fleshy plop.

"Fucking stupid," I whisper and doggedly refuse to focus on the fear and anger surging into my brain. Thinking about turning off the light cost me that one. I quickly sweep the ear onto the floor to join my other orphaned body parts and try to return to the vision of the unbroken me.

I succeed and time passes. It's hard to know how much.

I don't know how I ended up this way. Maybe it's some kind of virus. I've got a bit of an anxiety issue, so I spend a lot of time on the internet researching terrible diseases—mostly to see if I have any of the symptoms—but I've never heard of anything like this. Maybe it's a curse or something. I don't normally believe in that stuff, but for some reason I think about the old Russian guy who runs the laundromat. He yells at me because I take too long to dry my clothes. Sometimes, he yells at me in Russian, and it sort of sounds like a spell or incantation. Maybe he's a sorcerer or a wizard. He could have put the whammy on me because of that time I forgot my quarters—

My right shoulder is a white-hot mote of pain. My arm probably weighs fifteen pounds, and it makes a solid, meaty thud when it hits the floor. I don't look. If I do, it'll be all I can think about.

"I'm whole. I'm whole. I'm whole," I say aloud, almost chanting. The strange mantra pushes my thoughts back to the vision of the unified me, almost. It sounds like I'm saying "I'm a hole" over and over again. That's kind of funny, and—

Splintering pain inside my mouth. It feels like I've got an enormous semisolid chunk of bubblegum in there. I open up and my tongue falls out, hitting the carpet with a soft, wet noise. I taste the dirty shag for a split second.

"I'm ho. I'm ho. I'm ho," I sputter and then burst out laughing. This costs me two fingers on my left hand.

"I'm ho! I'm ho! I'm ho!" I shout now, desperate, trying to recapture the one thought that will halt my slow, bizarre dismemberment. I get there. I see the perfect, complete, and wholly intact me. I cling to it. I manage another indeterminate span of minutes without losing anything else.

My carefully cultivated focus is soon broken by the front door opening up the hall. My nose falls off. The carpet doesn't smell any better than it tastes.

"Randy?" My wife's voice drifts through the closed door of our bedroom.

"I'm ho! I'm ho! I'm ho!" I'm yelling at the top of my lungs now, although I can still hear fingers and toes falling onto the bed and carpet in rapid succession.

The door opens and my wife enters the room. Her scream rises above my shouted mantra, and it becomes the only thought in my brain. The room spins end over end, and it sounds like someone has dropped a bowling ball on the floor.

My head rolls across the room and comes to a stop at my wife's feet. I'm looking up into her widened eyes. I manage one more "I'm ho."

Side Effects

Harold approached the final electrical outlet in the living room, a roll of duct tape in one hand, his bottle of Clozaril in the other. He squatted down, squinting to peer into the topmost socket. Sometimes the little ones would wait inside and then jump out to bite you when you got too close. He didn't see anything moving, so he quickly ripped a strip of duct tape from the roll and covered both the top and the bottom sockets. So far, the duct tape had been effective; he guessed they weren't strong enough to push or chew through it.

That was the last outlet in the apartment, and Harold sat down in the middle of the living room to think about what he should do next. He'd already removed all the furniture; it was just too easy for them to hide under sofas, chairs, and tables. Or worse, a bed. He'd thought about ripping up the carpet—they could hide under there, too—but decided against it. The carpet was white, and that made it easier to see them when they crossed it.

He took a deep breath and popped open his bottle of Clozaril. The doctors told him it would keep him from seeing them. Just one little white pill a day. He'd been taking three or four, and still he saw them, still he heard them skittering and scratching behind the walls. He shook out a pill, put it into his mouth, and dry-swallowed it. Maybe it would work this time, or maybe he'd just have to come to grips with the fact that they weren't a product of schizophrenia, even if no one else would agree.

A dark shadow fell over the white walls and carpet of

the empty apartment. He looked up at the bare light bulb in the ceiling—he'd long since removed all the fixtures—and saw something moving within it. Pangs wormed their way into his guts, and there was sudden, urgent pressure on his bladder. One of the bigger ones had somehow gotten inside the light bulb, and it was jumping against the transparent surface, its many legs making a light tinkling noise against the thin glass.

Harold shot to his feet and ran into the kitchen. He grabbed the big, black flashlight off the counter and the only piece of furniture that remained: a small stepladder. Back in the living room, he set the ladder under the light bulb and switched on the flashlight.

He mounted the stepladder. The light made him squint, but it was the first time he'd seen one of the big ones up close. He guessed most folks would call it a spider, but that would be like calling a dinosaur a "lizard." The thing rattling around inside the light bulb had more than eight legs; Harold guessed it had over a dozen. Its entire body was covered in a jet-black shell, like the big scorpions he'd seen at the pet store. Then there was the *spider*'s head. It had only one eye, bright red and malevolent, and below that eye was a set of writhing mouth parts and a pair of white fangs half-an-inch long. It was about the size of a hummingbird.

The spider's movements had grown more frenzied, and it slammed itself against the thin glass. Harold sucked in a deep breath, drew back the heavy flashlight, and hammered it against the lightbulb. The glass shattered and he heard a thick pop as the spider was crushed beneath the blow. His flashlight not enough to hold that darkness at bay. He ran back into the kitchen and the welcome white glow of the overhead light. He flipped the flashlight around and saw that most of the spider's pulped body still clung to it. Its innards were pale yellow, like a mass of wet macaroni. He set the flashlight on the counter and wiped his hands on his jeans.

Now they were coming in through the light fixtures. What next—the plumbing? He guessed he might be able to stop up the toilets and sink. Thinking about it made his throat raw and scratchy, and he coughed. He coughed again, this time harder, spraying spittle across the kitchen. Still his throat itched, like there were tiny legs scratching at his esophagus.

He rushed from the kitchen into the bathroom and planted himself in front of the bathroom mirror. The itch in his throat was growing. He opened his mouth wide and looked inside. At first, he saw nothing but the pale-pink flesh of his tongue and gums—and then the first set of legs appeared at the back of his throat. He tried to draw in a breath, but his throat was suddenly clogged. He reeled away from the sink, clawing at his face. The spiders came pouring from his slack mouth, running down his shirt in a cascade of skittering legs and gleaming red eyes. He fell to his knees, choking, feeling dozens of tiny fangs. He fell forward, crushing spiders beneath his body, but still they flowed from his mouth. The bottle of Clozaril rolled from his pocket and spilled its contents across the floor. One of those white pills sprouted black legs and scuttled toward him, but his mouth was too full to scream.

144

The Grass Is Greener

Marcus put down the binoculars and pulled his mask aside so he could speak. His voice shuddered with excitement. "There's . . . there's grass down there."

"What?" Alex said. "That's not possible." He held out his hand and Marcus passed him the binoculars. He peered down at the orchard below the hill and saw rows of dead, skeletal trees. Between them was nothing but dirt and dust, and then, at the very edge of what he could see, a flash of green. His mouth fell open. Brown, gray, black: these were the colors of the new world. He had nearly forgotten what green even looked like.

"Do you see it?" Marcus said, eager and excited.

"I see something," Alex said, unwilling to entertain what that spot of color might mean. He didn't think he'd survive the disappointment.

"We have to check it out," Marcus insisted, then turned his head and coughed.

"Put your mask back on," Alex said. "There might still be vapors out here."

Marcus nodded and pulled the cloth mask back over his mouth and nose. The biological agent that killed every living thing ten years ago except a small number of lucky—some might say damned—humans had largely dissipated. There wasn't enough left to kill. Traces of it still lingered, though, especially in places that had once been fertile, like the orchard below.

"We're supposed to be getting food," Alex said.

"There's no food down there, and people are counting on us."

"But if that's grass, maybe we wouldn't have to eat out of cans anymore. Maybe we could grow things again," Marcus said. He was twenty-two and still had hope. Alex, at forty, his lungs riddled with lesions, his muscles wasted from lack of food and clean water, had only grim stubbornness to keep him going. But that flash of green in the binoculars kindled something warm and welcome.

Alex pulled the rifle from his shoulder and ejected the magazine. He didn't need to count. He knew how many rounds he had left. He counted them anyway, maybe just to give himself time to process what he'd seen. He rattled the eight rounds of 5.56 in his fist, then put them back in the magazine and loaded the rifle. "Okay, we'll go closer."

The lines around Marcus's eyes crinkled in a smile.

"Stay behind me," Alex said. They hadn't seen any other humans in months besides those in their tiny group of survivors. The last time they'd encountered others, Alex had fifteen rounds in his rifle. Some people didn't eat out of cans, and not because they grew their own food.

They made their way down the hill, moving slowly and deliberately so they didn't kick up dust. That's how you spotted someone in a dead world. Living things moved, movement made dust, and dust meant resources you could take—or eat.

The orchard loomed like a field of decaying giants, their wasted limbs reaching up to the sky as if pleading to a god who could not hear them. Alex kept the rifle at low ready, safety off. He could see the patch of green now, two hundred yards away. He kept his pace slow, even though his heart hammered with excitement, and, yes, he finally admitted to himself, with hope.

"Alex, look at it," Marcus breathed.

Alex nodded as the green spot grew larger, and he suppressed a smile behind his mask. He could now see individual blades of grass poking up through the dirt and detritus. God, could it be? Life finding a way to flourish through all this death?

They were ten yards away when Marcus' excitement got the better of him. He sprinted forward, pulling away from Alex when he made a grab at the young man. Marcus reached the patch of green, squatted down, and put a bare hand to the earth, then snatched it away. His eyes no longer shone with excitement.

"What is—" Alex's words were cut short by the thunder of gunfire. A single shot from the north.

Marcus flopped over, face-first, his limbs jerking spasmodically in sudden death.

Alex ran toward Marcus, knowing it was pointless, knowing he'd only join his young friend. Another shot rang out, and the bullet made a high whining buzz as it passed inches from Alex's head. He reached Marcus, saw the ragged exit wound in the young man's head.

Another shot blasted the breath from Alex's lungs as a bullet tore through his chest. He fell backwards with a grunt and dropped the rifle. He could now see the grass clearly, feel it beneath his hands. The green was too bright, too uniform. The blades bristling beneath his hands too firm and too sharp. Absurdly, he remembered a baseball game he'd watched in Tampa Bay before the world died. The game had taken place in a huge dome—the ruins of which lay not more than a few miles from the orchard—and had been played on a field of brilliant and artificial green.

Alex watched a group of a dozen men and women emerge from behind a crumbling stone wall about fifty yards away. They were gaunt, their clothing little more than rags, and they looked every bit as wretched as the decaying orchard around them. They carried an assortment of knives and axes and moved with a slow, feral caution. All but their leader. He held a rifle, stood tall and straight, and wore a tattered baseball cap, the stylized TB just visible beneath the dirt and grime.

The Inside People

Victor wiped the spittle from his mouth after another coughing fit and stared up at the tower. Alabaster white, it rose hundreds of feet in the air, a bastion of antiseptic purity in an ugly and dirty world. He stood in the manicured gardens at its base, the floating silver spheres of the automators keeping it green and healthy despite there being no one to enjoy it.

Through the sealed, shatter-proof glass at the tower's base, the interior of the ground floor shone with cleanliness: pristine marble, brushed steel, and white plastic.

Victor was keenly aware of the stink of his body, the way his skin itched beneath a layer of dirt he could never seem to wash off, and how his clothing hung on his body in drab, filthy folds. He wanted to walk through the translucent portal in front of him, out of his own decrepit, crumbling world and into the silent purity beyond.

He reached for the door.

"Careful!" a voice said from behind Victor. It was Horace, old and wily. Only he had been brave enough to accompany Victor to the tower. The rest were still afraid of the inside people, though they hadn't seen one in weeks. "There might be an alarm or something."

"We need food. There's none out here, so it must be in there."

Victor pushed open the door. No electric jolt struck him dead, and no alarms sounded. It wasn't even locked.

He stepped into a world forbidden to him his entire life. From his earliest memories, there had been the inside people who lived in the towers and the outside people who survived beyond their gates.

Victor had lived his whole life combing the garbage pits for food, listening to the ceaseless rumbling from the automated factories, and living with the sounds and stinks of his fellow humans. The interior of the tower smelled, shockingly, like nothing, and only their careful footsteps made any noise.

"Where do they live, Victor?" Horace asked and broke into a coughing fit. He hacked up a thick wad of phlegm and spat it onto the white marble floor. Everyone had been sick, much worse than usual. Many had died, but it had eventually passed.

Victor pointed to the ceiling. "Up."

The ground floor was smaller than Victor expected, and they found only two doors: a wide, silvery one with buttons and a plain one hidden away in an alcove beside it. They couldn't open the first door; pressing the buttons had no effect. The second, however, opened onto stairs. They climbed three flights before they came to a long hallway with thick, white carpet, white tiles on the walls, and more doors, each with a silver number stenciled on its surface.

Victor stopped at a door marked with the number 100. He pushed it open, surprised that it was unlocked. Beyond was a small, metal room. An empty white suit and a clear plastic helmet hung from hooks on one wall. The suit gave Victor pause, as did the slight stink of rot, but they had come too far to turn back.

From the metal room they entered a large, square chamber with an alcove in one corner that held shelves piled with plastic boxes and bags. The room was filled with furniture in silver and white: chairs, benches, and sofas made of cushioned leather and cloth. Victor had only ever sat or slept on concrete with little between his flesh and the cold. The urge to experience comfort nearly overwhelmed him. Before he could sit, a soft mechanical noise drew his attention to the other side of the room, to another door standing slightly ajar.

Victor followed the noise and stepped inside a small room dominated by an immense bed, upon which lay the corpse of a man in a shapeless white gown. The smell of rot was strong here. A tall machine stood next to the bed, and tubes ran from the machine to the corpse, disappearing under the gown. The machine made the noise Victor had heard. It sounded like breathing.

Victor had never seen an inside person outside of his suit. The man had no hair and no beard, and his skin shone alabaster and unblemished like the great tower he'd lived in. His limbs were thin and spindly, his head bulbous, the eyes too large, the nose too small. The sickness had killed the man. The old, dried vomit on his mouth and the red-brown stain on the bed beneath him told Victor as much. He'd seen many of his own people die the same way.

Looking at the corpse of the inside person, Victor remembered something his mother had told him when he was a child. She'd said for all their towers and machines, the inside people were weak. He'd never believed it. The inside people were gods, untouchable and immortal. But here one lay, covered in his own shit and vomit, slain by the same death that had claimed many of Victor's people and all of his.

Horace entered the room behind Victor, both hands laden with plastic bags and containers, his mouth full of the food within them. He swallowed and joined Victor next to the bed. "If there's no one here, can we be the inside people?"

"Go tell everyone to come and help us take the food from this place," Victor said.

"But why? Can't we live here?" Horace said, crestfallen.

"No." Victor drew the sheet over the dead man's face. "The inside people are dead."

Toward the Sun

We walked toward the sun, orienting ourselves when it was lowest in the sky, figuring that would lead us west. We walked beside dead fields of wilted brown, cracked riverbeds that held only dust and bones, and the scorched concrete monoliths of sunbaked cities.

There were five of us when we set out from Boston, three men and two women. We each carried the weight of lost children and loved ones left drained of moisture and life in houses and apartments little more than heat-scorched tombs. Five strangers brought together by the sun grown red and massive, beginning its death throes billions of years ahead of schedule. Our star faced the end with haughty pride and refused to give up its bright throne in the sky.

The sun shone nineteen of twenty-four hours when we started our journey. The few hours of darkness offered brief respite from the murderous glare and triple-digit temperatures. Those hours waned the further west we traveled. By the time we passed St. Louis, the sun only sank below the horizon for a scant three hours.

A faint hope the Pacific Ocean would offer sanctuary pushed us on. One of us, Dr. Ephraim Adams, a tall, strangely cheerful man who'd taught environmental science at Boston University, told us it would be simple to set up a desalination process. We'd have all the water we needed. I doubted him because I'd seen the scorched plain of the Atlantic. Maybe there was still water out there in the middle of all that desolation, a once-mighty ocean reduced to shallow puddle. Not that it mattered; the heat would bake your insides before you'd gone ten miles.

We scavenged water where we could from small reservoirs in toilet tanks or the occasional cache of water bottles, half-evaporated, warm and awful on the tongue. The water ran out in Las Vegas and reduced our number to four. A small, pretty woman named Jolene Hanson simply sat down in the middle of I-15, the heat mirage rising around her in stifling waves. She looked up at me and smiled. "That's it, Sam. I'm done."

No one argued with her. We understood. I looked back once after we'd left. I'll always remember Jolene staring up at the sun, dead sunflowers beside the road nodding toward her like a line of mourners at a funeral.

The next night, Jamal Holbrook lay down with the rest of us in the fleeting, hazy darkness. The gunshot jolted us all awake. We didn't have the strength to bury Jamal, so I took the gun from his stiff hands and we continued on.

It grew cooler in the Sierra Nevadas, and I wondered if maybe that great expanse of dark blue water would greet us when we came down from the mountains. I dared not hope, but Dr. Adams assured us the cooler temperatures meant the ocean still lapped at sandy shores, cold and vast.

We found an overturned Alhambra truck beneath an overpass in Central California that had evaded looters. The relative cool beneath the overpass had preserved two five-gallon jugs of pure water. We sat in the shade and drank our fill, reveling in something like joy or maybe just appreciation for a slight reprieve before the end. Perhaps we should have conserved the water, but if the Pacific was dry, I wanted to die with spit in my mouth rather than the dust I'd breathed for three thousand miles.

In Modesto, California, about ninety miles from the coast, our numbers fell to two. In the empty tomblike silence of a shopping mall, Rebecca Lucas met her end. We'd been dragging our water behind us in a child's wagon. Foolish, but we'd stopped believing there were any other people left, let alone any people who would harm us. When we stopped to rest and drink, the three men who had been following us attacked.

They shot Rebecca while she sat beside the wagon, drinking from her canteen. The bullet went through her and into one of the big Alhambra jugs. It spewed water tinged pink onto the tile floor in a steady gush, and that's all that saved us. Dr. Adams and I ran, abandoning the wagon. Our attackers were more concerned with the water spilling onto the ground than pursuing us, and we escaped.

Thirty miles from the coast, Dr. Adams started talking to himself. Ten more miles and he began to shout long strings of scientific formulae interspersed with peals of high-pitched laughter. I ignored him for as long as I could, and then, when I could take it no longer, I shot him. I shot him because I wanted quiet. I shot him because I knew he'd lied about the ocean in the west. I shot him because I wanted to die alone.

I arrived in the seaside town of Carmel exactly three hundred days from when I'd left Boston. I passed through empty streets that had once moved to the slow rhythm of crashing waves and delighted visitors with the stinging scent of brine. I heard nothing but the wind. I smelled only dust and my own rancid body odor.

When I reached the beach, it was not empty. Others had heard the myth of the Pacific and traveled west. Their bodies lay in the sand, burnt and rotting. I saw gunshot wounds in the bleached skulls of half a dozen. Others, like Jolene Hanson, had sat down and died quietly, their corpses folded around a loved one or perhaps just a surrogate stranger.

The ocean bed stretched on endlessly. A new sea of gray silt, but if I stared long enough at the heat waves rising from over it, I could see blue, hear waves, smell the salt in the air.

I saw footprints heading off into the mirage, dozens and dozens of them. I followed, walking toward the sun, always toward the sun.

About the Author

Aeryn Rudel is a writer from Tacoma, Washington. He is the author of the Acts of War trilogy of novels published by Privateer Press, and his short fiction has appeared in *The Molotov Cocktail*, *On Spec*, *Pseudopod*, and many others. Aeryn is also a notorious dinosaur nerd, a baseball connoisseur, and he knows more about swords than is healthy or socially acceptable. He frequently documents his authorly musings and dubious advice on writing and rejection (mostly rejection) on his blog at www.rejectomancy.com or Twitter @Aeryn_Rudel.

About the Artist

Valerie Herron is a Pacific-Northwest-based illustrator of the mythological, the macabre, and the absurd. She received her BFA in Illustration at Pacific Northwest College of Art in Portland, Oregon.

Valerie has illustrated numerous books, including *The Book of the Great Queen* by Morpheus Ravenna, as well as two Lovecraft anthologies—*The Book of Starry Wisdom* and *The Book of the Three Gates*—by Strix Publishing. Valerie has created art and content for multiple entertainment media enterprises, such as RiffTrax, Faerieworlds, Privateer Press, and Pacific NorthWEIRD.

Outside of her creative practice, she spends her time listening to music and podcasts, being out in nature, playing with her animals, writing, reading, gaming, and exploring a myriad of sorcerous activities.

Publishing Notes

"Things That Grow," first published in *The Flame Tree Fiction Newsletter*, Flame Tree Press, 2021

"Shadow Can," first published in *The Molotov Cocktail*, 2014.

"The Sitting Room," first published in *The Molotov Cocktail*, 2016.

"Two Legs," first published in *The Molotov Cocktail*, 2018.

"The Rarest Cut," first published in *EGM Shorts*, 2015.

"The Last Scar," first published in *Trembling with Fear*, 2018.

"Second Bite," first published in *MetaStellar*, 2020.

"Ditchers," first published in *Aphotic Realm,* 2019.

"An Incident on Dover Street," first published in *The Molotov Cocktail*, 2017.

"Small Evil," first published in *The Arcanist*, 2019.

"Time Waits for One Man," first published in *Factor Four Magazine*, 2018.

"Simulacra," first published in *Ellipsis Zine*, 2018.

"Reunion," first published in *The Arcanist*, 2017.

"When the Lights Go On," first published in *The Arcanist*, 2018.

"Far Shores and Ancient Graves," first published in *New Myths*, 2019.

"Little Sister," first published in *The Molotov Cocktail*, 2017.

"The Night Forever and Us," first published in *Love Letters to Poe*, 2021.

"The Father of Terror," first published in *The Molotov Cocktail*, 2016.

"Stall Number Two," first published in *Ellipsis Zine*, 2020.

"Do Me a Favor," first published in *The Arcanist*, 2018.

"Where They Belong," first published in *DarkFuse Magazine*, 2016.

"Night Walk," first published in *The Molotov Cocktail*, 2015.

"The Thing That Came with the Storm," first published in *The Molotov Cocktail*, 2019.

"Masks," first published in *The Molotov Cocktail*, 2016.

"Cowtown," first published in *The Arcanist*, 2017.

"Bear Necessity," first published in *The Molotov Cocktail*, 2018.

"The Grove," first published in *The Molotov Cocktail*, 2019.

"Beyond the Block," first published in *The Molotov Cocktail*, 2015.

"A Man of Many Hats," first published in *The Molotov Cocktail*, 2016.

"His Favorite Tune," first published in *The Flame Tree Fiction Newsletter*, Flame Tree Press, 2020.

"At the Seams," first published in *The Molotov Cocktail*, 2014.

"Side Effects," first published in *The Molotov Cocktail*, 2015.

"The Inside People," first published in *Ellipsis Zine*, 2018.

"Toward the Sun," first published in *The Molotov Cocktail*, 2020.

Jacket art, *Night Walk*, by Valerie Herron, 2021.

Antler Bart, by Valerie Herron, 2020. Reproduced by permission of the artist.

The Marsh, by Valerie Herron first appeared in *The Book of Starry Wisdom*, Strix Publishing, 2016. Reproduced by permission of the artist.

Gemini, by Valerie Herron, 2018. Reproduced by permission of the artist.

themolotovcocktail.com

Printed in Great Britain
by Amazon